Praise for RITA® Award-winning author Helen Brenna

"Brenna's book offers a riveting plot and sparkling dialogue."
—*RT Book Reviews* on
Along Came a Husband

"I laughed and I cried over this book, and it holds a very special place in my heart, as I am sure it will in yours!"
—*Romance Reviews Today* on
Then Comes Baby

"This book is enchanting."
—*Love Romances and More* on *Then Comes Baby*

"Be prepared for romance, suspense and a lot of emotion from this beautiful book."
—*Cataromance* on *Next Comes Love*

Dear Reader,

I knew when I was writing Maggie Dillon and Nick Ballos's story, *Finding Mr. Right,* that little sister Kate was going to eventually need her own story. I didn't know it would involve Riley. Now that it's all done and written it makes so much sense! Turns out they were destined to be together from the moment their names first appeared on the same manuscript page.

A little note about the plot. As I'm known to do, I've fudged a bit. Yes, there are, depending on the version of mythology, up to ten Greek primordial gods. While I've done my best to make sure all the names I've mentioned are mythologically accurate, there are not ten known statues of these gods from the Hellenistic period scattered around the world. Sure made the story fun to write, though.

Three more Mirabelle Island stories will be coming in 2011. Sarah Marshik is going to knock heads with (yes, finally!) one of Garrett Taylor's brothers, there's a new bed-and-breakfast owner coming to town and Missy Charms's sister, Marin, finds herself in need of a little R and R. Only, Mirabelle has a few surprises in store for her.

I love hearing from readers, and I answer all correspondence. Drop me an email at helenbrenna@comcast.net, or send a letter to P.O. Box 24107, Minneapolis, MN 55424.

My best,

Helen Brenna

The Moon That Night
Helen Brenna

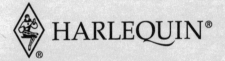

TORONTO • NEW YORK • LONDON
AMSTERDAM • PARIS • SYDNEY • HAMBURG
STOCKHOLM • ATHENS • TOKYO • MILAN • MADRID
PRAGUE • WARSAW • BUDAPEST • AUCKLAND

Recycling programs
for this product may
not exist in your area.

ISBN-13: 978-0-373-78417-2

THE MOON THAT NIGHT

Copyright © 2010 by Helen Brenna

ABOUT THE AUTHOR

Helen Brenna grew up in central Minnesota, the seventh of eight children. Although she never dreamed of writing books, she's always been a voracious reader of romance. So after taking a break from her accounting career, she tried her hand at writing the romances she loves to read.

Since she was first published in 2007, her books have won many awards, including Romance Writers of America's prestigious RITA® Award, two *RT Book Reviews* Reviewers' Choice awards, the Holt Medallion and the Book Buyers Best Award.

Helen lives with her family in Minnesota, and she'd love hearing from you. Email her at helenbrenna@comcast.net or send mail to P.O. Box 24107, Minneapolis, MN 55424. Visit her website at www.helenbrenna.com or chat with Helen and other authors at RidingWithTheTopDown.blogspot.com.

Books by Helen Brenna

HARLEQUIN SUPERROMANCE

1403—TREASURE
1425—DAD FOR LIFE
1519—FINDING MR. RIGHT
1582—FIRST COME TWINS*
1594—NEXT COMES LOVE*
1606—THEN COMES BABY*
1640—ALONG CAME A HUSBAND*

HARLEQUIN NASCAR

PEAK PERFORMANCE
FROM THE OUTSIDE

*An Island to Remember

For Tina Wexler

Just because

Acknowledgments

I'm so fortunate to be surrounded by smart and cultured princesses. It seems at least one of them has a hand in helping me get my facts straight in each of my books. This time it was Warrior Princess Zena, aka Tina Plant, aka Valentina Anatolievna. Thank you, sweetie, for helping me with all things Russian. Maybe someday we'll go to Moscow together! Oh, and she never makes mistakes, so you may trust that any you find are all mine.

Thanks, as always, to Johanna Raisanen for her editing insight.

And last but never least, my unending gratitude to Tina Wexler for being such a great cheerleader, a joy to work with and for helping me make every book better.

CHAPTER ONE

"GET BACK OR GET DEAD." Riley inserted a detonator into a small amount of C-4. "I'm blowing the door." While he preferred all the assholes surrounding him dead, that particular objective would have to wait. He spun around the dark corner. "When this goes," he said to the supreme asshole behind him, "we'll have less than five minutes to get the statue and get out of here."

"You're really going to pull this off, aren't you?" David March said, grinning.

"What has to be done gets done."

"The consummate soldier." March chuckled. "I knew you were the best man for this job."

When this was all over Riley was going to show March what being best was all about. He turned as the small explosion blew the lock to smithereens and the door swung open.

March pointed to Riley. "Clear the room."

A cloud of smoke and tiny particles of debris

hung in the air, making it impossible for Riley to see more than several inches in front of his face. Slowly he stepped across the threshold. From nowhere a chair came at him. He put up his hand, grabbed the leg and yanked it away. The unknown attacker screeched. A woman. *Perfect.*

Wrapping his arms around her midsection and pinning her hands at her sides, he quickly immobilized her. Although they'd anticipated someone could be working in the room, they hadn't expected any resistance, and he sure hadn't expected to feel curves this nice on the likes of a museum curator.

"Let me go, you big ape!"

The woman struggled against him, but despite the fact that she had fairly well-defined muscles, there was no contest. A good foot shorter than him and little more than a hundred pounds, she was about as much trouble as a pesky gnat buzzing around his neck.

"Who are you?" she yelled. "And what do you want?"

That voice. Something about the surly tone had a distinctly unpleasant familiarity. He was frantically trying to make the connection when the woman slammed her heel down on top of his foot. "Enough," he said quietly, despite the fact that his foot now throbbed. "I'm not going to hurt you."

As the smoke cleared, he let her go. She spun

around and wound up, preparing to wallop him. The sight of her—pale skin contrasting with dark hair and golden-brown eyes firing as bright as a sunlit tiger's eye—hit him like a rubber pellet to the chest, knocking the wind from him and leaving him totally unprepared. "Kate Dillon?"

Her fist connected with his diaphragm, and he sucked in a breath. For a lightweight she packed one hell of a punch.

"Riley?" Surprised, she jumped back and studied him. "Is that you?"

It might have been almost ten years since he'd last seen her, but a man didn't easily forget a girl like Kate. She'd been all of about seventeen years old and a pistol then, too. One little stint as a bodyguard during a personal leave and he'd been more than happy to get back to active duty. He and Kate hadn't seen eye to eye on anything, and while he would've liked nothing more at the time than to tie her up and put a muzzle on that sassy mouth, she'd been a job. He'd promised to protect, and protect is what he'd done for three hellish days. And nights.

Back then she'd been attractive in a promising sort of way, but he'd never been into robbing cradles. While her youthful beauty might have turned into an I-eat-men-for-midnight-snacks kind of allure, with no makeup and her hair bunched in two short, braided pigtails she looked as if she still couldn't walk into a bar and order a beer without getting carded.

"What are you doing here?" he asked, glancing at his watch. Time was ticking.

"Shouldn't I be asking that? You just blew off my door."

He glanced around the room. A lab of sorts. "You're working here, aren't you?"

"What's it to you?"

Surprise, surprise. Her mouth and attitude hadn't improved. Double the reason he'd never made a move on her all those years ago. Not only had she been too young, she'd also been too outspoken for his tastes.

As far as he was concerned, women were supposed to be soft-spoken and compassionate. A woman should complement her man, not compete with him. He wasn't a chauvinist, simply a realist. Throw together two people who were too much alike, and instead of harmony all you'd get was chaos. There was no doubt in his mind that Kate Dillon plus a man like him equaled chaos times ten.

"What do you do here?" he asked.

"At the moment, restoration work. Why?"

This was too much to be a simple coincidence, but it still didn't make sense. "March!" Riley called. "You coming or not?"

March came into the room, followed by a couple

of his goons, including Mick Coben, his right-hand man. "Good job," March said to Riley before fixing his gaze on Kate. "Hello, Miss Dillon."

"Who are you?" she asked.

"David March. A great admirer of your work." He glanced around the room, his gaze landing on the obviously old statue on the nearby table. "What do you need to finish repairing that piece?"

"Why?"

He glared at her. "I don't have time for this."

She glared back at him. "And I'm supposed to care?"

"No." In one surprisingly swift movement, March was by her side with the barrel of his gun pressed against her temple. "But I'm guessing you care about making it out of this building alive."

Riley pushed March's gun toward the ceiling, and Coben made a threatening step forward. "Back off, Coben," Riley said.

March gave a short nod, and Coben reluctantly stepped down.

"She wasn't part of the plan," Riley said.

"Of course she was." March grinned. "Kate's a night owl, aren't you? Especially when she's on deadline to get repairs finished before an exhibit opens."

She only narrowed her eyes at March.

Son of a bitch. The pieces were starting to fall into place in a twisted David March kind of way.

That man had been a thorn in Riley's side ever since they'd done their first tour of duty together in the Gulf War. Sometimes he wondered if he was ever going to be rid of the unprincipled a-hole.

"I'll handle Kate." Riley bit out the words.

"You have one minute." March stepped back. "Then things go my way."

"Kate, listen to me." Riley turned her to face him. "These guys aren't messing around."

"Excuse me, but aren't you one of *these* guys?"

"I don't have time to explain—"

"Well, that's—"

"For once in your life, girl, could you do what you're told?"

"I'm a woman," she snapped. "Not a girl. Thank you very much."

Coben chuckled softly. "Can't handle her, old man? Need help, let me know."

Riley might be a bit worse for wear after twenty years in the marines, but it'd be a cold day in hell he couldn't handle this little spitfire, let alone the likes of Coben. "Kate, I'm only going to ask you this once." He jerked his head toward the work in process on the table. "What do you need to finish your repairs on that piece?"

"Nothing," she said through clenched teeth. "I was basically finished with it."

"What do you typically need to repair this type of statue?" March asked.

"Why?"

"Kate," Riley said softly, "answer the question."

"Clay," she said. "Some tools and adhesives."

"That's it? You're sure?"

"Yes," she hissed.

"Get those supplies together and let's go."

She didn't move.

"Now." Riley grabbed her by the back of the neck and pushed her toward the reddish-brown clump of clay on the table. "The man isn't kidding about putting a bullet in your head. Got it?"

Her cheeks turning an angry red, she stuffed a hunk of clay into a thick plastic bag. After grabbing a handful of tools from the workstation and some small containers of paint and glue, she snatched up a shoulder pack. "Now what?"

March ignored her and reached for the ancient-looking statue she'd been working on. "Can't forget this."

"Don't touch that!" One of the goons grabbed Kate's arms and held her back. With one quick twist she shook him off and grabbed the statue. "This is a fragile, authentic Greek figurine from the Hellenistic period. It's about twenty-five hundred years old."

March grinned. "I'm well aware of that."

"It may be priceless in terms of historic value," she muttered, "but it's certainly not worth this effort."

"That, dear Kate, is a matter of opinion."

Riley's watch beeped, signaling thirty seconds before the guards would hit. "We gotta get out of here."

"Give me that statue," March said, ripping it out of her hands.

"No!"

"Grab her."

Gripping Kate's arm, Riley dragged her out of the room. They'd no sooner closed the door on the stairwell than security guards rushed into the hall behind them. March's men laid out a burst of rapid fire, stalling the onslaught.

Down three flights of stairs, through a maze of hallways, and past a ghostly quiet shipping and receiving area, Riley pushed through a back door and into the chilly November night air. Since he'd knocked out the streetlights earlier, the only illumination in the alley came from a hazy moon. The van, lights off, was idling only a few feet away.

March climbed into the vehicle. "Get her in here," he called to Riley. "Now!"

Angry and exhibiting not the slightest bit of fear, Kate glared at him. "You're really going to kidnap me?"

Life from Riley's perspective was straightforward

and simple, every decision black and white. This was as clear-cut as it got. Without an ounce of remorse he stared back at Kate and ground out, "Get in."

CHAPTER TWO

POSITIONED TIGHTLY between two of the jerks who had robbed the small museum she worked for occasionally, Kate sat on her butt across from Riley, swaying to and fro as the van hightailed it through the streets of Washington, D.C. A burst of cold autumn air traveled up her back, sending a shiver down her spine. Figured. She would manage to get kidnapped and thrown into the back of a van without a jacket during a record-setting November cold snap. As escape options quickly flicked through her mind, her gaze clashed with Riley's.

"Don't even think about it," he said, low and deep.

If he was even as half aware of everything going on around him as she remembered, there was no way she was getting out of this vehicle. "You used to be one of the good guys." She glared at him. "But then, maybe that was all a lie."

A couple of the other men laughed. The instant Riley turned his gaze on them, they quieted. All but one. A man just as big as Riley, if not bigger, sneered at him. "Full of bullshit," the man said. "That's about right."

"Coben," Riley said, "when this is all over, you and I are going to settle a few things."

"Why wait?" Coben snickered.

Interesting. No love lost between those two.

March glanced back from the front passenger seat. "Knock it off."

Riley's gaze, as unreadable as ever, flicked toward Kate. After all these years she couldn't believe she still remembered Riley, but what woman ever forgot the most irritating man she'd ever met?

When her sister, Maggie, and Maggie's now husband, Nick, had run into some trouble in Greece several years back, Riley had escorted Kate back to the States and acted as her bodyguard for several days. Not only had he stuck to her like slip on clay, he'd barely spoken the entire time. Although one-word grunts had been the extent of his side of their limited conversations, his disapproval of her—her appearance, her life, her opinions—had rolled off him like twenty-foot waves.

If the disdainful look in his eyes when he glanced her way was any indication, his assessment of her hadn't changed. Neither had he. Still cold, silently focused and built like a linebacker, he wasn't handsome in a traditional sense. But with his features—eyes as blue as a cobalt glaze, sharply bowed lips and a cleft in his chin partially hidden by several days of stubble—God help the women of this world if Riley ever chose to smile, let alone laugh.

He sure hadn't even come close to cracking a smile during the entire three days he'd been her bodyguard all those years ago, and still she'd found herself viscerally attracted to him. He'd been her first major-league crush, the first man—not boy—to make her pulse race and her skin burn.

She'd been too stubborn to admit to her teenage self that back then he'd completely intimidated her, but the truth was if she hadn't been scared to death of the way he'd made her feel, she might've been nicer to him. Then before she'd had a chance to come to grips with her strange feelings, he'd left. Mission accomplished. Time for new orders. She'd been so insignificant to him she'd been shocked he'd remembered her name.

So what had happened to him that he'd sunk to kidnapping and theft?

The moment Riley turned his attention toward the front, she slowly reached into her pack, felt around for her cell phone and hit the emergency call button.

Riley immediately grabbed her arm and tore the phone from her hand. Without a word, March took the cell from Riley and set it on the console in front of him.

"I can't believe you're doing this." She stared at Riley. "What do you people want from me?"

He looked away.

None of this made sense. "That one clay statue isn't worth this trouble," Kate whispered.

"By itself, no," March said. "But put it with the others and the collection is priceless."

Whether or not a collection actually existed was debatable, but many experts believed that a small rosebud carved into each of several ancient statues now located in various spots around the world indicated they'd been made by the same nameless artisan, something that was extremely unusual for the time period in which they'd been created.

"So that's what this is about?" she said. "You're going to steal the other primordial deity statues in that set?"

Most people were familiar with the Olympian gods of Greek mythology—Zeus, Aphrodite and the like—but many had never heard of the first-born gods, those said to have actually created the universe. Gods like Gaia, Nyx and Tartarus, the gods of earth, night and the underworld. There were others, too, depending on the stories to which a person subscribed. Some writings told of as many as ten such primordial gods.

The statue Kate had been working on at the museum, Erebus, the god of darkness and shadow, was a spectacular piece. If more had been discovered created by the same artist...

"You're too smart for your own good," March murmured as his cell phone rang.

"But—"

"Someone shut her up!" March ordered, putting his cell phone to his ear.

Riley put out his arm, stopping one of the other men from reaching for her. His black long-sleeved shirt stretched tight as the muscles in his chest and arms tensed. "Kate?" he said. "Can you manage that on your own, or will I have to shut you up myself?"

She put her hand over her mouth and glowered at Riley.

"I don't care how you manage it, just get it done," March said into his phone before disconnecting the call.

She tried to keep her head about her, tried to pay attention to where they were going, but from the rear of the van it was difficult deciphering street signs. A short while after they'd left the museum, the vehicle pulled up to a gate and they drove into what looked like a private underground garage.

Someone opened the back van doors, and fluorescent lights beamed inside. She squinted against the sudden glare as Coben yanked her out of the vehicle. A blast of cold air hit her, sending a trail of goose bumps over her arms. With Riley following, she was led to a large table.

"Sit," Coben ordered.

"Screw you."

"I got a better idea." Leering at her, Coben trailed his hand along her shoulder and over her arm. "Maybe *I'll* screw you."

"Coben, give it a rest," Riley said, his tone soft and menacing. "And Kate." He took a chair across from her. "Sit down and shut up."

The fact that Riley didn't need to raise his voice, let alone flex his obvious muscles, to exude strength and power unnerved Kate. Jerking away from Coben, she dropped onto the chair as March came to the table.

"Time to unveil the rest of my plan." March set the statue of Erebus on the table along with her pack filled with the clay from the museum and her tools. "But first I must give credit where credit is due. Kate, you hit the nail on the head." He smiled at her, then turned to Riley. "You're going to help me steal the rest of these statues."

Silently Riley held March's gaze.

March slid a file and a cell phone across the table and directly in front of Riley. "That's everything you need to know, and then some. Locations, floor plans, security system details. You will check in as you go."

Riley ignored the file, but he was clearly getting angrier by the second.

Only half listening, Kate looked for an escape route. It was only Riley, March and Coben in the room. The other guards had disappeared. Her best bet was likely the stairwell on the far side of the garage, but where did it lead? If she could get to the van she might have a chance. If March's men didn't shoot her or the tires out first. If the keys and a garage door opener were in the van. If—

Who was she kidding? There was no chance she was going to make it to that van, and even if she did, what was the likelihood she'd make it out of this building? Still, she couldn't just sit there.

"This is all very interesting," she said, standing. "But since you don't appear to need me—"

"Sit down," March ordered.

"I want out of here, and I want out now!"

Coben came behind her, twisted one of her braids in his hand and tugged downward. It hurt like crazy, but Kate had a feeling one way or another she was going to end up dead. If she didn't make a stand now, soon there'd be no point. As hard as she could, she swung her elbow backward, connecting with Coben's gut. Twisting away from him, she ran two steps toward the van before Coben grabbed her arm and yanked her back.

"Bitch!" He grabbed her by the throat.

"Coben." Riley pushed back from the table. "Let her go."

Kate couldn't breathe. She struggled and clawed at his hand, but nothing she did had any effect on the monster.

"That will do, Coben," March said calmly.

Coben forced her back onto the chair before finally letting go of her throat. She sucked in a breath and caught Riley's gaze. Although he looked as if he was ready to kill Coben, something was holding him back. What? Why was he doing this?

"Kate," March said. "You must understand. Until I decide it's time to let you go, the only way you're getting out of this building is with a bullet in your head."

And that was that. She did her best to hold back a rising sense of panic while March went on as before.

"I want you to tackle the easiest target first," March said to Riley. "The Church of Sant'Aurea in Ostia Antica, about fifteen miles southwest of Rome. They don't know what they have on their hands, so stealing those two particular statues should be a piece of cake."

"Did you say two statues?" Kate asked, feeling her jaw drop. This was impossible. "In Italy?"

March smiled. "That's right. Word is some grave diggers found them in a cemetery in town. Nyx and Hemera."

The goddess of night and her daughter, the goddess of daylight. If this was true, it was an amazing find. "By the same artist?" she asked.

March nodded.

He was right. If all the primordial deity figurines had been found, then the collection would be priceless.

"Now may I continue?" March asked with more than a touch of sarcasm as he turned back to Riley. "The second target will be a bit trickier. Although this statue is displayed in a private home in Athens, there are at least six armed guards surrounding the estate at all times. The owner is Angelo Bebel."

Riley snorted and shook his head. "Figures."

Kate recognized the name. Nick, her brother-in-law, was old friends with Bebel. The Greek was the one who'd sent Riley to protect Kate.

"You never know," March said. "Ask nicely enough and Bebel might give you his statue of Chaos."

The first of the primordial gods, the god of nothing and everything, the creator of the cosmos. Kate had only seen pictures of this figure, the most spectacular of them all. To hold the artifact in her hands would be incredible.

"Angelo's not going to hand over the statue," Riley said. "And you know it."

"Then you'll have to take it. The approach is entirely up to you," he said. "The last two statues will be the most difficult of all. They're in a private collection. In Moscow. Very well guarded."

"So that's what this is all about." Riley shook his head. "You can't go into Russia."

"You know Grigori," March said, snickering. "Now, there's a man with no sense of humor."

"You bastard." Riley stood to pace. "You don't have the balls enough to do your own dirty work."

"Why should I when I can get you to do it for me?"

"Grigori Kozmin swore he'd kill both you and me if we ever put one foot on Russian soil. If he finds out I'm in Moscow, I'm a dead man."

"You'll have to make sure he doesn't find out."

Riley glanced at Kate for a moment before returning his focus to March. "Well, Kozmin sure doesn't care about art, so who do the statues belong to?"

"*Belong* is a relative term. They are currently in the possession of Vasili Belov."

"The Russian mafia boss." Riley shook his head. "You really are a pansy ass, aren't you?"

March shrugged. "You say pansy. I say you're better than me at breaking and entering."

"What makes you think I won't be missed at the Pentagon?"

"Call your CO," March said, all humor gone.

"You've had a family emergency and are taking a personal leave."

"Is that it?" Riley asked. "Anything else you'd like me to take care of for you while I'm at it?"

"No, that should do it."

"And while I'm sweating bullets trying to pull this together you'll be, let me guess, sitting back sipping on a rum punch on some tropical island."

"Don't I wish, but my buyer's in a hurry. He needs this collection by next week and there are four other statues that need stealing besides the ones you'll be responsible for," March said, glancing at Kate. "Isn't that right, Ms. Dillon?"

She kept her mouth shut. Ten gods, so theoretically ten statues in the complete set.

"I'll be heading to Japan for two of them," March went on. "Then there's one in China. And the last is in Turkey, near our final meeting place in Istanbul."

"So you know where they all are and you've got a plan to steal them," Kate said. "What do you want from me?"

"Simply one week out of your life."

"To do what?"

"Well, that should be obvious. Museums, as well as individuals, have been known to put replicas on display, and you, Kate, are an expert on Hellenistic pottery." March walked to the stairway and yelled up to the first floor. "Stanley! You're needed down here."

A moment later a small, anorexic-looking man with glasses came down the stairs.

"This is my expert on Hellenistic pottery, Stanley Manning." March handed him the Erebus statue. "Real?"

While closely examining the statue, the man turned it over and over in his hands, paying particular attention to the rosebud formed in the figure's robes. "Yes. This is authentic."

"Good. Stanley will be coming with me. Kate, you'll be going with Riley to verify the authenticity of the statues he steals. It doesn't hurt that your restoration work is amazing. If anything should happen to any of the statues along the way, you'll be repairing them."

"No, I won't." Kate shook her head. "I'm not doing anything for you. And I am definitely not going anywhere with Riley."

"Yes." March studied her, and the predatory look in his pale gray eyes was almost enough to make her look away. "You are. And you will check in with me along with Riley at each location. I insist."

"Why should I?"

March opened a folder, withdrew a small stack of photos and flicked one at her. "Your sister Shannon is married to Craig Stanton. They have two children." The picture showed Shannon and her family laughing as they exited a movie theater. "Here's Maggie and her husband, Nick Ballos. Three kids." He flicked another photo at her depicting Maggie, Nick and their kids coming out of their home in Bethesda. Nick had his arm around Maggie's waist and was planting a kiss on her cheek. "Tessie, Daniel and Liam. Cute kids. Perfect families. Too bad."

Kate stared at the photos and felt a pain as sharp as if her heart was being ripped out of her chest. Ever since her mother had died so long ago, when Kate had been only eight, she'd yearned for her own family, for a house filled with a husband and kids, the sound of banter and laughter. She'd ached for that long-gone sense of place and belonging, would've given about anything for the opportunity to carve out her own piece of heaven. To imagine this man might destroy what Maggie and Shannon had somehow managed to build for themselves...

"Leave them alone," she whispered.

"I'm afraid it's too late for that, Kate. My men nabbed Maggie's oldest, a first grader, I believe, as the child was leaving school today."

Tessie. Oh, God. Staring at March, Kate pushed back from the table. "You're an animal!"

"Not really. But for ten million dollars, any man will push himself as well as others to the limit."

"And your cut?" Kate glared at Riley. "I hope it's worth it."

Colder and more focused than even March, Riley held her gaze.

For the first time since this nightmare had begun Kate felt her control slipping. She could deal with anything these men dished out for her, but Tessie? *Oh, Tessie.* She'd babysat her niece and nephews just last weekend while Maggie and Nick had taken a break in Cape Cod. The couple had come back looking relaxed and happy and more in love than ever. This would destroy them. They had to be out of their minds with worry.

March pushed back from the table. "So that's it. You two are booked on the first flight to Rome in the morning."

Coben yanked Kate from the chair.

"Hold on." Riley stood. "I want to see Jenny and Ally."

March considered him for a moment. "Five minutes. Maybe some time with them will provide you with some…incentive."

With Riley following, Coben shoved her into the elevator. As they went up two flights, Kate was too preoccupied with thoughts of Tessie to resist. The moment the door opened, he pushed her down a hall. One of the guards unlocked a door and forced her into a furnished bedroom. A four-poster king-size bed and large dresser. A sitting area with two chairs, an entertainment center and a table and lamp.

A woman, a gorgeous, blue-eyed blonde, looking to be in her mid-thirties, stood alert but quiet in one corner, her arm jutting protectively in front of a young girl by her side. They looked even more frightened than Kate felt.

Kate swung back around in time to see Coben and the other three men in the hallway point their guns at Riley. "When this is all over," Riley growled, "you're all dead."

"Yeah, yeah, Mr. All-Talk-And-No-Action," Coben said, motioning with his weapon. "You got five minutes. You wanna waste them out here in the hall, it makes no difference to me."

Riley backed up, and the guards slammed the door, locking him inside the bedroom.

"So you're not working with them?" Kate stared at him. "Then why did you take my cell phone?"

The woman in the corner ran forward, barreled full blast into Riley and hugged him. "Are you all right?" he asked.

The fact that a man like Riley had a significant other surprised Kate even more than she'd expected. She hadn't taken him for anything other than a man with a gun, a soldier through and through.

"I'm all right." The woman stepped back, her hands trembling. "You?"

"Fine." Riley set the woman away from him and glanced at Kate. "My sister-in-law, Jenny."

So Riley had a wife, or was Jenny a brother's wife? Kate had a feeling it would be best to wait with the questions, given this woman's state of mind. Jenny's face was a mass of emotions. Clearly she was tired, scared and confused.

"I'm Kate Dillon." As Kate gave the other woman a reassuring smile, the adolescent girl, who looked to be no older than thirteen, with long, silky blond hair, stepped out of the shadows to stand next to Jenny.

"And my daughter, Ally," Riley said.

Riley had a daughter? The reality wasn't computing. But then, she supposed, once was all it took to get pregnant, and women made mistakes all the time. "Hi, Ally." Kate smiled reassuringly at the young girl. "I'm Kate."

Ally nodded.

"I took your cell phone," Riley explained, "because March would've killed them both if anything had gone wrong with tonight's operation."

"I thought you were in on this," Kate whispered, turning to him. "Why didn't you say something?"

"Like I care what you think? Besides, it's not like we had a lot of time or privacy to discuss the situation."

He had a point.

"James, what's going on?" Jenny asked.

James? Go figure. While knowing his first name didn't soften Riley's image one iota, watching him with his sister-in-law did. He rubbed one of her shoulders as he quickly explained why Kate was here and March's plans to have him steal the statues. What didn't make sense was the way his daughter kept her distance.

Kate recognized that distrustful and obstinate look in the young girl's eyes. The kid was scared out of her mind and too tough to show it. Kate hadn't been all that different herself at thirteen, but then with a father who'd hit the road before she'd been born and a mother who'd died before Kate was Ally's age, who wouldn't expect a rocky road? Maggie and Shannon had done their best to raise Kate after their mother had died, but they'd both been teenagers, too. No wonder Kate had felt a little bit lost ever since her mother's death. She couldn't help but wonder about Ally's story.

Kate turned toward her. "You okay?"

"Oh, sure." The young girl shrugged. "I get kidnapped every day."

"You'll certainly have a story to tell the kids at school."

As Ally's thoughts apparently turned to friends, her eyes watered.

"Scared, huh?" Kate smiled. "Me, too."

Ally looked away.

"Honey, it's going to be okay." Riley put a hand on his daughter's shoulder, but she shrugged back and went to Jenny's side.

Riley clenched his jaw and said, "We're breaking out of here tonight. One way or another."

"How?" Kate asked.

"I'll take care of it." He turned toward her. "By the way, I think March is bluffing about your niece. I don't think his men have her."

"Tessie? How do you know?"

"On the way to the museum earlier tonight, he was on the phone. I didn't understand the one-sided conversation at the time, but now it makes sense. From what I heard, apparently your niece didn't go to school today. She was sick. So as long as we get out of here tonight, you'll have time enough to warn your sisters."

Footsteps sounded in the hall. They were coming for him.

Riley focused on Kate. "Sit tight, and wait for me. *Don't do anything.* I mean it."

The door opened and three guards stood in the hall. "Time's up."

Keeping his distance, Coben pointed his semi-automatic at Riley. "Let's go."

Riley studied his daughter's face, clearly looking for any sign of warmth, any crack in Ally's tough veneer. When the young girl stiffened, his shoulders imperceptibly sagged. He glanced at Jenny and silently mouthed, "Tonight" before leaving the room. The door shut after him and a lock turned with a resounding click.

CHAPTER THREE

Monday, 1:05 a.m.

"IF YOU ASK ME, THE word *tonight* implies before midnight." Unable—unwilling—to sleep, Kate paced the length of the large bedroom, her patience, what little she normally possessed, long since gone. She glanced at her watch. "So unless he's stuck in another time zone, your brother-in-law is late by more than an hour."

"James will do everything in his power to get us out of here," Jenny said quietly.

The woman had more confidence in Riley than Kate was ever likely to have in any man, her own brothers-in-law excluded. "Well, I'm sick of sitting around waiting. What do we need him for, anyway? There's got to be something we can do to get out of this place."

"Like what?" Ally sat up in bed, hope lighting her eyes.

"You got any ideas?"

"They have us locked down tight," Jenny said politely. "It's not happening."

With that vote of confidence, Ally hung her head in defeat.

"Besides, James told us to sit tight," Jenny went on as if she hadn't said enough already. "He'll come for us."

"And if he doesn't?"

"James says what he means and means what he says. He must be waiting for an opportunity."

"See, that's my point. What if an opportunity never presents itself?" As far as she was concerned, they were on their own. "Maybe we're the ones who are going to have to save Riley," she said, stopping in front of one of the windows to glance outside into the chilly fall night.

They were being held on the second floor. Through the bare branches of a tall maple she found Connecticut Avenue stretched out below them, a few of its townhomes already bright with lights in preparation for the upcoming Christmas holiday. Cars zipped back and forth. A lone man, head down, walked his Doberman along the sidewalk. She jumped up and down. Waved. Nothing. She could stand there naked and it wouldn't make a difference.

She tried opening the window. Nailed shut. If she broke the glass, the guard would hear. Getting more pissed off by the minute, she stalked across the room. For the fourth time since they'd taken Riley away a couple of hours ago, she yanked on the doorknob, and for the fourth time, the door didn't budge.

"Damn it!" She pounded on the solid wood. "Let us out of here!"

"This is your last warning," said the guard stationed outside in the hallway. "Shut. Up."

"Or what? You going to come in here and make me, tough guy?"

"I wouldn't do that if I were you," Jenny whispered from where she sat on the bed. "There's no point in making them angry."

"Maybe not, but it sure does make me feel better." Kate eyed the room, taking it apart piece by piece. A clock. Lamp. Picture frames. Books. None of it of any use. They hadn't cleared out the room before throwing them in here probably because they didn't see three females as much of a threat. They probably weren't, but she had to try. "There's got to be something in here I can use as a weapon."

Ally picked up the brocade coverlet on the bed. "We could throw a blanket over them, like a net."

"Good idea, Ally, but we're not tall enough or big enough to hold them down."

"What about this table?" Ally asked.

Kate glanced at the ornately carved wooden legs. "Too heavy, I think, but wait a minute." The photo frame on the bedside table caught her eye. Metal.

She snatched up the picture, took the frame apart and broke it at the corners. The resulting point was quite sharp.

"You made a knife." Ally smiled.

Kate was beginning to really like this kid.

"What are you doing?" Jenny asked.

The sister-in-law, on the other hand, had no spine as far as Kate was concerned. "I'm going to try and get out of here." She wasn't deluding herself into thinking she could take down the guard outside their door, but she *could* distract him.

"Be careful," Jenny said.

Kate would rather be dead than careful. "I'm going to draw the guard into the room and create a diversion. You two take off out the door."

"What about you?" Ally asked.

"Don't worry about me. Flag down a car as soon as you get outside and call the police."

"But I can help," Ally said. "I need something I can use to hit him."

"Ally, don't you dare," Jenny whispered. "You stay out of this."

"Just because I'm thirteen doesn't mean I can't help."

"But you could get hurt," Jenny whispered.

"Kate can't do this alone," Ally insisted.

"All right," Jenny said. "Find something I can hit him with, but you stay out of this, Ally."

"That's not fair." Ally glared at her aunt. "It was my idea."

"Ally, sit," Jenny ordered. "On the bed."

Kate wholeheartedly disagreed with Jenny treating her niece as if she was helpless, but it wasn't Kate's call. "The chairs in here are too heavy." She stalked into the bathroom and spun around. "A towel rack. Yes!" After yanking the rod out from between the two brackets, she handed it to Jenny. "When he comes through the door, hit him over the head or on the back."

Kate hid the makeshift knife behind her and pounded again on the door. "Hey!" she called. "Let me out!"

"Okay, that's it," the guard mumbled. A key sounded in the lock.

"Get ready," Kate whispered, but Jenny looked scared stiff. She might be beautiful and congenial, but Kate had a feeling the woman was going to be useless.

"I told you to shut up," the guard said, coming toward Kate.

Jenny didn't move. Kate was going to have to do this alone. Quickly she swung her arm out and jabbed the corner of the picture frame into the guard's gut. The metal grabbed.

"Son of a bitch." Disbelieving, he looked down at his stomach. Blood seeped through his shirt.

"Jenny, hit him!" Ally called out.

"No, go!" Kate yelled as the guard lunged toward her.

Jenny grabbed Ally and tugged her toward the door.

Kate swung again at the guard. He grabbed her wrist, wrapped his other arm around her and yanked her to his chest, immobilizing her.

"Leave her alone!" Ally pulled away from Jenny and jumped on the guard's back.

"Stop right where you are!" That was Coben's voice. "Or Jenny's dead."

Kate stilled and glanced up. Coben had a gun pointed directly at Jenny. Kate dropped her makeshift knife. "Ally," she whispered. "It's over."

The other guard knocked Kate to her knees. "The bitch stabbed me!"

"Serves you right." Coben pushed Jenny to the other side of the room. "You. Troublemaker." He pointed at Kate. "Get up and come with me."

ON EDGE AND CHILLED nearly to the bone, Riley eased himself up from a sitting position on the damp concrete floor and stretched out his stiff legs. He glanced through the barred egress window facing the alleyway. They'd taken him down into the garage level and locked him in one of the back rooms. Judging by the position of the nearly full moon, it was probably around the 1:00 a.m. mark. Too soon to attempt anything.

Voices sounded in the hall and he grabbed the length of metal he'd dislodged earlier from one of the shelving units and positioned himself to take advantage of any opportunity for escape. Keys sounded in the lock, and Riley cocked his arm as someone was pushed through the partially open door and into the dark storage room.

"Get your hands off me!"

Great. Just what I need.

At the sound of Kate's voice, Riley lowered his makeshift weapon. The door closed and the lock was quickly turned. Not only had he been offered no chance to take out one of the guards, but he was also now saddled with Miss Mouthy.

"Is someone in here?" she whispered, her vision likely not yet adjusted to the darkness of the room.

"Behind you."

She spun around, wrapping her arms around herself. "Riley?"

"Who else were you expecting?" He leaned the bar against the wall. "Let me guess. You tried to escape."

"Hell, yes!" With her hair disheveled, one braid all but out and the other seriously frayed, she looked wild. Moonlight flashing in her golden eyes and highlighting her full lips only added to the effect. "I'd attack that guard again, too, given the opportunity."

It shouldn't have surprised him. "I asked you to sit tight."

"Like a good little girl?" She huffed, her left eyebrow arcing and a pair of dimples popping as she flattened her mouth. Pulling off the dangling binders holding together what was left of her braids, she ran her fingers through her dark shoulder-length strands. "Like that'd ever happen."

Suddenly she looked a lot more dangerous than at seventeen. The obstinate gleam in her eyes brought to mind a disturbing—at least for him—occurrence from years back when he'd acted as her bodyguard.

Late the first evening they'd been settling in for the night at her and her sister's apartment in D.C. Clearly forgetting he was present, Kate had come out of her bedroom in only a bra and thong, stopped dead in her tracks on seeing him, and stood there for a moment before brazenly continuing on her way into the bathroom.

She might have been only a teenager back then, but the girl had more balls than a lot of men he knew. Try as he might, Riley hadn't been able to take his eyes off her, and he'd ended up feeling like the scum of the earth for it, too. He'd been pushing thirty at the time, so the very last thing that should've been on his mind was a seventeen-year-old woman child.

Unfortunately he still remembered the exact

blue hue of her undergarments and the way that color had perfectly offset her creamy skin and dark auburn hair, her pink lips and rich amber eyes. Not to mention perfectly matched the sexiest set of tattoos he'd ever seen. Tiny, bright blue butterflies in various stages of flight not only encircled her left wrist, but a cluster of them stretched from under her breast along her side and onto the edge of her back.

He swallowed, pushing aside the memory.

"So now instead of a nice cozy bed and warm covers," he said, "you're treated to cobwebs and cold concrete. Satisfied?"

"I'd be more satisfied if you'd made good on your promise to escape tonight."

He'd surely never met a more contrary and infuriating female, so why did he have the urge to—God help him—silence that mouth with a kiss? He shouldn't be attracted to her. And he sure shouldn't be bothering with the verbal sparring. It was getting him absolutely nowhere except possibly turned on.

He shook his head, hoping to knock some sense into his brain. "For your information, Kate, the night is not over. It so happens one against five ain't the greatest of odds. Even for me. I'm waiting for the guards to settle in." He went back to the corner he'd previously been sitting in and crouched down to stay warm. "I suggest you make yourself comfortable and get some sleep. I'll wake you when it's time to move."

"There's no way I can sleep." Rubbing her arms, she paced.

He stared at her left wrist, wondering if he might get a glimpse of those butterflies. Not happening. She wore a leather-banded watch that hid every single last one of them.

"It's too cold in here," she breathed.

He sure hoped she didn't expect him to do anything about that particular problem. Talk about a recipe for disaster. A grizzled old soldier like him, brushing up against the nubile likes of her. In the dark, no less. Then again, a guy could dream, couldn't he?

"I'm sure the second-floor bedroom March claimed is plenty cozy," he muttered.

"Whose house is this, anyway?"

"Who knows? March more than likely simply took over a vacant location that suited his needs." He tried to avert his gaze from her silhouette, but since she was standing in the stream of moonlight, it was hard not to notice the way her cargo pants hugged her bottom or the way her tight green T-shirt formed perfectly to the curve of her small breasts.

Hunks of dried clay clung to her pants and the bottom edge of her shirt. There was even a gray smudge along the edge of her cheek. Take in the entire package and there was something so…earthy about her. Earthy and solid. For some unaccountable reason, he felt a pull toward her like gravity.

"You don't like me very much, do you?" she asked.

The question caught him totally off guard. At the moment he was liking her too much. "Why do you say that?"

"From the first day I met you at Angelo's back in Greece all those years ago, you've shown nothing but disdain for me. With your words, your actions, how you look at me."

"Let's just say I'm not used to being…challenged." And challenge him she did, on many levels.

She seemed to be weighing his response, and while she didn't appear completely satisfied, she didn't look quite sure about how to pursue a line of attack. "You still in the military?"

He nodded. "Marine Corps. Been on active duty for most of the last twenty years." Probably would be for another twenty, too, unless he signed those early-retirement papers that had crossed his palms three months ago.

That'll be the day. Once a soldier, always a soldier.

"Then what are you doing in D.C.?"

"Routine rotation out of Afghanistan. Been consulting for the Department of Defense for the last several months."

"So if you're such a good guy, then how do you know March?"

Riley sighed and closed his eyes for a moment. If this topic wasn't enough to douse the sudden fire sparking inside him for Kate, then nothing would. "I met him a long time ago. We went through boot camp at the same time," he started. "Did our first tour of duty together in the Gulf War. Desert Storm. We ended up on the same team, wet behind the ears and looking to be heroes. It was March, Roy Abrams and me."

"I'll bet the writing was on the wall even back then," she said, leaning back against the door.

"Actually, it wasn't. At least not right away. But then a few months after we got there, we were in Kuwait, part of the liberating forces. March picked a fight with an Iraqi soldier we'd cornered on reconnaissance. The guy went for March, but Roy got in the way. Stabbed in the neck."

"Did he die?"

"Bled out in the dry dust and dirt." Riley looked away. "After that, March started losing it one tick at a time. I don't think anyone noticed but me."

"Something had to send him over the edge."

"That happened some years later. His little brother Alex was captured by insurgents in Iraq. We searched for him for days. Had a line on where they might be holding him, but there were too many civilians in the area to stage an all-out rescue attempt. March volunteered to go in alone, but they wouldn't let him. Too personal. So I went. Only, Alex wasn't there."

He paused, took a deep breath. "The next day we found his body hung in pieces off a bridge. March held himself together. Or so it seemed. But when they sent us to Kosovo to be part of NATO's peacekeeping force, little by little March stopped toeing the line." Riley shook his head. "Before I knew it, I was bailing him out of one mess after another.

"Then one weekend, we were on furlough. In a bar having a few drinks. Before I knew it, March was gone. Out the back door. I found him in an alley a couple blocks away with four guys surrounding him. Like an idiot, I ran into the fray, thinking he needed help. Turns out he'd pilfered a couple M-16s, a grenade launcher and a sniper rifle and was doing a deal."

Kate stood silent, listening.

"I figured I was dead. March, too. That's when I met Angelo Bebel. He and a couple of his men came out of the back door of some warehouse, armed and ready for a fight. Angelo was setting up some trade agreement that apparently had gone bad. It didn't take much to convince the arms dealer to take his weapons and hit the road. That was that."

"I can't believe Angelo helped out and he didn't even know you."

"Don't kid yourself. Angelo and I might've become fairly good friends after that. I even spent quite a bit of time at his home in Athens and his place on the island of Patmos. But Angelo doesn't do anything that doesn't benefit him in some way. He figured if he helped out a couple U.S. Marines, we'd come in handy some day. March didn't, but I did."

"What happened to March?"

"They kicked him out. BCD."   At her puzzled look, he explained. "Bad conduct discharge. The only reason he wasn't court-martialed was because they couldn't pin any missing weapons on him. But March never forgave me for testifying against him. After that he started blaming me for everything bad that ever happened to him. Roy Abrams. The deal going bad in Kosovo. Even what happened to Alex."

"So that's why he kidnapped Jenny and Ally?"

"As far as he's concerned, this is payback."

"How did you end up at Angelo's shop when I was there with Maggie all those years ago?"

"I was stationed in Afghanistan at the time. Angelo called in his favor. Asked me to help him get some precious-gem inventory he'd already paid for out of the country. I took a short furlough, brought him his inventory and happened to be there when you showed up at his shop. If you'd come in the day before or the day after, we never would've met."

"Until this."

"Apparently." He glanced at her and shrugged. "March made his plans independent of you and me. The fact that I knew you was an added bonus for him."

"Then it seems one way or another," she whispered, "we were fated to meet again. It's odd to think Ally was about three when we first met," she said, smiling. "I never would've guessed you for a father."

He said nothing.

"Is Jenny a brother's wife, or—"

"My wife's sister."

"So then…where's your wife?" she asked softly.

CHAPTER FOUR

AT THE MEMORY OF AMY, Riley turned away. "She died when Ally was born."

"I'm sorry," Kate whispered, briskly rubbing her arms as if struck by a sudden chill. "How did it happen?"

He would have thought that after thirteen years the pain would've subsided, but no. Maybe pain didn't really begin to explain how he felt when he thought of Amy. Remorse, regret, guilt. He hadn't been able to fix her, hadn't been able to protect her. In fact, he'd been directly responsible for her death. Never before or since had he felt that same level of helplessness.

"Riley?"

He glanced at her. "The details are really none of your business."

"If it had anything to do with March, it's my business."

"Amy never met March. Her death had nothing to do with him, so it has nothing to do with you."

"Okay."

Clearly it was not okay as far as she was concerned. He could add nosy to the quickly growing list of her annoying attributes. No doubt the subject of Amy would come up again.

She paced as goose bumps broke out on her arms. "What about this Russian? Grigori…"

"Kozmin," Riley said. Back on safe ground. "I was in Georgia, training NATO-led forces for deployment to Iraq. Kozmin's girlfriend worked at the military base. That's how I met him. One day March shows up in town. Before you know it he's messing around with Kozmin's woman and gets caught screwing her in the back room of some bar."

"That explains why he wants March, but how did you get involved?" Her teeth chattered as she shivered in the cool, dank air.

And, no, he was not going to warm her up. "I got involved by accident. Walked into that very same bar and found Kozmin about to kill a man with his bare hands. The guy was so bloodied I didn't even know it was March. While I was holding on to Kozmin, thinking I was doing him a favor by keeping him out of prison, March slipped out the back door."

"So now Kozmin will kill you if he finds out you're in Moscow."

"He won't find out."

"You sure about that?"

He needed to shut her up, so he could rest his eyes for a few hours. "The only things I'm sure of is that I'm all done answering questions, you're cold and the last thing we need to deal with is you going into shock from hypothermia."

"I'm fine." She wrapped her arms more tightly around herself.

"Come here," he said, spreading his arms and legs to make an opening for her in front of him.

"I'm supposed to snuggle up? With you?"

"You want to get warm or not?"

For a moment she debated, the expression on her face running the gamut from confused to relieved. What did she think he was going to do, attack her? Then maybe she didn't trust herself. In the end, the promise of his body warmth was clearly too inviting. "All right, fine. But no touchy feely, okay?"

"Okay."

As if she was afraid of second-guessing herself, she quickly scooted down and backed against his chest. He rested his arms on his legs, making sure to keep his hands clear of any inappropriate contact.

Kate sighed. "My God, you're like a human furnace."

"You, on the other hand, are an icicle." He'd bet his last dollar, though, that she was anything but an ice queen under normal circumstances.

He took a deep breath, her small body heavy

against his chest. It was a surprisingly nice feeling, her slight but solid weight against him. *Don't go there, old man.*

"So we're clear," she said. "This doesn't mean anything, so don't get any ideas."

Too late. As she pressed back against his chest, his legs, his groin, all kinds of *ideas* were racing through his mind and not a one was polite enough to share.

THE MAN WAS AS HARD as granite.

Then again, he felt a touch too soft to be likened to a rock, but too hard to be made from mere flesh and blood. Kate sat between Riley's legs, the heat of his big body slowly seeping deeper into her back, arms and straight into her core. She sighed and relaxed against him.

Only, relaxing wasn't the only thing she was doing. She wasn't seventeen anymore, and now that she knew he was really on the good side of the law, that crazy crush she'd had on Riley all those years ago seemed to have matured into something much less innocent.

His arms rested on his knees, but it was obviously not a comfortable position for him. Occasionally his hands slipped and hit the cold concrete floor. Finally he said, "I…need to rest my hands on you."

"Whatever's comfortable."

He moved his hands to her waist, and then as if that were too intimate a location, he went to her shoulders. That positioning seemed worse, so he rested the backs of his hands on her thighs.

"Oh, for crying out loud." She grabbed his beefy fingers and pulled them in to her waist. "This is a simple exchange of heat. Nothing more. Nothing less."

"If you say so."

She didn't just say so. She would make it so. The last thing she needed in her life was another man who so clearly disapproved of her. *Challenging,* he'd called her. Well, more than likely, just like every other man who'd gotten to know Kate, Riley could write a list a mile long of all the things wrong about her. She might not have yet hit thirty, but she'd already accepted that she'd likely never have what her sisters had. A family, a home, a husband and kids? *Not gonna happen.* Wanting something wasn't enough. Not for Kate.

Years of dating one man after another had proven without a shadow of a doubt that she wasn't, never would be, girlfriend let alone wife material. Guys liked soft and sweet. Nurturing and obliging. Everything Kate wasn't. And there was no way she was changing for a man.

That didn't mean she couldn't take advantage of the proximity of a hot-blooded male like Riley. He was, without question, the warmest body she'd ever felt. His arms at her sides created a comfortable half cocoon as his chest at her back rose and fell in a steady, slow rhythm. Soon enough, her eyelids grew heavy, and Kate—for the first time in her life—fell asleep in a man's arms.

RILEY GLANCED at the location of the moon through the window. Probably around four. Chances were that anyone who was going to fall asleep had already done so. It was time to move.

He glanced down at Kate's profile. She was sound asleep, her head lolling back against his shoulder. Funny, in this state, her lips parted, relaxed and blissfully quiet, she actually looked docile. What a beautiful sight. Too bad he couldn't sit there and enjoy the image a while longer.

But then, the *image* wasn't the only thing he wanted to enjoy. Take that long length of creamy-white neck, for example. He'd bet anything her skin would taste as sweet and warm as she looked. And that cleavage, just enough to get a man wondering…

A pervert. That's what he was.

With her warm body snuggled against him, it was difficult keeping in mind the fact that she wasn't much more than a kid. Not only didn't she feel like a kid, she didn't smell like one either.

The scent of something clean but feminine wafted through his senses. It was all he could do not to imagine her in a bikini with a large flower in her hair. Wouldn't that be a sight? With those butterflies along her side, making it look as if they might pick her up and carry her into the air?

She shifted, slumping down, and his hands were suddenly in contact with the lower swell of her breasts. She wasn't voluptuous, but there was plenty there to make his fingers itch to inch upward, to hold her slight fullness in his palm. Then it wasn't only his fingers but his entire body becoming acutely conscious of how she pressed against him.

Yep. Perv. Through and through.

Time to get a move on. "Kate," he whispered in her ear. "Wake up."

A small sigh escaped her as she shifted onto her side, snuggling into him even more closely. Her breast landed in the palm of his hand and he closed his eyes for a moment, using every ounce of restraint to keep his thumb from gliding over her nipple. He jiggled his hand free and tapped her arm. "Kate?"

She startled awake, managing to elbow him in the thigh. Damn, she was strong.

"Shh," he whispered. "Relax."

She stilled.

"It's time to go."

"Okay," she murmured. Running a hand over her face, she stood.

His backside cold as stone, he slowly unfurled

his stiff limbs and stood. One of his knees was aching and his arm had fallen asleep, but he'd manage. Quietly he opened the window and tore out the screen. The bars were meant to keep people out not in, but there was no way he could squeeze himself outside through that thin space. Still, Kate might've been able to manage it and he needed the guard distracted for only a second.

"What are you doing?"

"Hoping the guard thinks you escaped through the window."

If Coben came to the door, Riley would need something more than an open window to buy him some time. If more than one guard showed up, the only chance he'd have was if they were under orders to shoot to maim, not kill. He picked up the metal bar he'd earlier leaned against the wall.

"I want to help," Kate whispered. "What do you want me to do?"

"Stay behind me. I don't want to have to worry about protecting you."

"But—"

"Give it a rest, Kate." Making as much noise as he could, Riley knocked over a storage shelf and then, shoving Kate behind him, hid in the shadowy corner to wait for the guard.

It wasn't more than a few seconds before the door cautiously opened. Two guards, guns drawn. *Not good.* The front man glanced inside, noticed the open window and took a step into the room before realizing his mistake. Riley swung the metal rod, knocking the guard out cold. The other guard, a young guy, pointed his gun at Riley.

"Not supposed to shoot me, are you?" Riley said, egging him on.

"That doesn't mean—"

Riley kicked the gun out of the man's hand, spun and swung his foot higher, knocking him to the floor and disorienting him. Then Riley grabbed the guard's handcuffs, gagged him and secured him to one of the window bars.

"Grab the guns," he whispered to Kate. He took the keys, locked the guards in the room and with Kate following moved quietly down the hall.

They were in luck. There was no one else in the glass-enclosed security room, so no one was left to monitor the security cameras. Quickly and quietly, avoiding the elevator, they made their way up the stairs to the main level of the building. This was a private residence, a town house, and a well-appointed one at that. Shouldn't have surprised him. March always had liked luxury.

"I'm going upstairs to get Ally and Jenny," he whispered.

"What about the statue?" Kate asked.

"What about it?"

"You don't understand. If the Erebus statue I was working on is truly part of a complete set from the

Hellenistic period, this would be an important discovery. I have to find it. I can't leave it with March
and take the risk it's destroyed or disappears."

Of all the... "You're kidding, right?"

"I won't make a sound. I swear." She walked
away before he had the chance to grab her.

Arguing with her was only going to wake someone. "I'm getting Ally and Jenny," he whispered.
"When I get back, you'd better be ready to go, or
we're leaving without you."

While Kate searched the formal living room,
Riley crept up the next flight of stairs. He encoun-
tered no one as he went to the room where they
were keeping the girls. Carefully he unlocked the
door. Two figures lay still on the bed.

Quickly he woke Jenny. "Shh," he whispered in
her ear. "Let's go."

As she jumped up next to him, he went to Ally's
side and nudged her awake. "Ally," he whispered.
"It's Dad. Wake up."

Going perfectly still, she stared into his eyes.

"Be quiet, okay? We're getting out of here. Come
on."

"Where's Kate?" Jenny asked.

"She's downstairs looking for her precious
statue. Let's go." He led the way to the main floor.
"Kate?" he whispered.

Nothing. He couldn't see her anywhere. Of all
the obstinate, single-minded women he'd ever

met, she took the cake. Well, Kate Dillon could no doubt fend for herself for a few more hours. He led Jenny and Ally down into the garage. "Get into the van."

"What about Kate?" Ally whispered.

"After I get you two safely out of here, I'll come back for her."

"You can't leave her here," Ally said.

Oh, yes, he could, and that was exactly what he was going to do. Besides, March wouldn't hurt Kate. The man still needed her.

"I don't believe you." Ally crossed her arms. "You'll leave anything behind, won't you?"

That cut deep. His decision to leave his daughter with Jenny after Amy died had been one of the hardest Riley had ever made, but he'd had to accept his own limitations. It was a man's duty to serve his country and provide for his family. It was a woman's job to hold that family together. A soldier had no business raising a child, let alone a baby. As difficult as it had been, he'd done what was best for Ally.

"Listen—"

"She's right," Jenny whispered, laying her hand on his arm. "We have to get Kate."

"Jenny, I don't know where she went." With Ally and his sister-in-law in tow, he couldn't go traipsing around the house looking through every room.

"Well, she couldn't have gone far," Jenny said.

"You stay with Ally." Before he could stop her, Jenny was heading up the stairs. "I'll be right back."

What was with all these headstrong women? "Get in the van, Ally." He quietly opened the passenger door.

"But Dad—"

"But nothing. We need to be ready to move."

Ally climbed inside, leaving the door open, and a moment later Kate came down the stairs. "I couldn't find the statue."

"Where's Jenny?"

"She's not with you?"

"She went looking for you." They'd quietly passed each other without realizing it. "Get behind the wheel," he ordered Kate. "Start up the engine and get the van ready to move out of here. I'll find Jenny."

Kate climbed into the driver's seat, and he'd taken no more than a few steps when the elevator chimed, signaling the doors were about to open. "Kate!"

"I'm on it!" She started the van and positioned the vehicle for a quick exit.

"Ally, get down on the floor!"

The elevator doors opened and March and Coben stepped out, guns drawn. And they were holding Jenny.

CHAPTER FIVE

"GET OUT OF THE VAN!" March yelled. "Now!"

Gunshots rang out a warning. They were jacked. Either he, Kate and Ally got away now, or no one did. For an instant, Riley caught Jenny's gaze. *Somehow, someway, I will make this right.*

"Go, Kate!" he yelled, running toward the open passenger door. "Drive!"

"But Jenny!" Ally screamed. "We can't leave her, Dad!"

"We don't have a choice." He climbed into the van and slammed the door. "Hit it!"

She punched down the accelerator, crashed through the garage door and swerved onto Connecticut, barely missing an oncoming car. "Now what?" she asked, her eyes wild with panic.

"Just drive! Get the hell out of here as fast as you can."

"Dad, we have to go back," Ally cried.

"I will, Ally. We get you two safe, and I'll go back for Jenny."

A cell phone rang inside the van.

"That's my cell phone." Kate glanced at him, surprise registering.

The thing was sitting on the console where March had left it last night. Riley snapped it open.

"Close but no cigar." March's voice came over the line. "You may have gotten away with Ally, but I still have Jenny, so nothing's really changed, has it? You *will* steal the statues. Exactly as I laid out for you last night."

"Like hell."

"You owe me, Riley," March said softly. "For Alex."

"Alex wasn't my fault."

"That's a matter of opinion. Besides, you're stuck. Coben will be on your tail in two minutes to keep an eye on you, so don't even think about doubling back for Jenny. Make any attempt to rescue her, and she's dead."

Damn it! He had no choice.

For now.

"All right, March. I'll get you the other statues, but make no mistake. You hurt one hair on Jenny's head, and I promise that your death will be the most agonizing experience known to man."

"Right. Coben's got your passports, tickets to Rome, Kate's pack of pottery supplies and my files with the documentation on the statues. When you get to the airport, he'll give you everything you need and then make sure you get on the plane to Italy. When you arrive in Rome, I expect you to check in with me. Both you *and* Kate," March said, stressing the last.

"Let me talk to Jenny," Riley said. "Please."

A short moment of silence hung on the line before Jenny came on. "James?"

"Jenny, I'm sorry."

"You did what you had to do. Ally's safe."

"I'm going to get you out—"

"Meet me in Istanbul." March was back on the line. "Next Saturday by midnight with all five statues and Jenny will be fine. I'll call you later with the details, but know this. For every hour you're late in Turkey, your sister-in-law will suffer the consequences."

"When this is over," Riley said, "I will be coming after you."

"Save it," March said. "You have six days left, and your clock is ticking. Istanbul. One week. You try and screw me in any way, my deal is off and your sister-in-law is dead."

A heavy silence filled the air inside the van as March disconnected the call. The sky was only beginning to brighten as sunrise approached.

"I heard everything," Kate said. "What do you want me to do?"

Riley's thoughts raced, considering alternatives.

He had none. "Head to the airport. For now I have to follow March's orders."

"You can't leave Jenny!" Ally screamed through tears. "You have to go back for her!"

"Ally, don't." He glanced back into her face, his heart breaking for the pain and accusation in her eyes. "I don't have a choice."

"I hate you," she whispered. "Even more than before."

It was all he could do not to hop into the back and hold her. She might be thirteen and think she knew every little thing there was to know, but Ally was still a kid, and kids needed to know they were safe. And loved. That's why he'd left her with Jenny in the first place. Not to mention the fact that having a baby in the house was exactly what Jenny had needed after her sister had died. "Ally—"

"Don't!" Ally made a show of plugging her ears. "Don't even try to explain. I'm not listening."

Snapping his mouth shut, he turned to the front.

"You should've taken Jenny and Ally and left," Kate whispered. "Jenny shouldn't have come back for me."

"Trust me. It wasn't my idea."

"I'm sorry."

Sorry wasn't going to cut it.

"Kate, pull over!" he called as they approached a twenty-four-hour drugstore. "Right there!"

Coben might be catching up to them, but they were ahead by a few minutes, and a few minutes was all this stop would take. He hopped out as she approached the curb, ran into the store and bought several disposable cell phones and calling cards. Then he ran back outside.

Coben had pulled up behind Kate and was already climbing back into his car after presumably handing off her pack, their passports, tickets and other documentation Riley would need. "Get a move on, Riley!"

Riley ignored him and climbed into the van.

Kate didn't say a word, only drove back out into traffic and headed for the airport.

Riley opened one of the cell phones and dialed a number, keeping his fingers crossed his call would be answered. He could organize a crew of good men to take March down and extract Jenny, but he didn't have the luxury of that kind of time.

Finally the call was picked up and a groggy voice mumbled, "This better be good."

"Trace?"

"Riley?"

"It is you." Riley breathed a sigh of relief. Thank God he hadn't changed his number. Trace was the only person in the D.C. area Riley knew who could move fast and do the job right. The man might have lost a leg in Afghanistan, but that wasn't going to hold Trace back.

"What's going on?"

"You always said you wanted to return the favor I did for you in Guatemala." Until Riley had shown up, Trace had been about to lose a hand and then some in a poker game gone bad. "You ready?"

"It's about time. You name it, it's done."

Riley quickly gave his old buddy the details. He wasn't happy about having to take Ally along with him to Rome, but at least then he'd know she was safe.

"So March still has Jenny?" Trace asked.

"Yeah. He'll likely move her ASAP."

"What do you want me to do?"

"I CAN'T BELIEVE IT!" Kate hung up the cell phone as she followed Riley and Ally through the airport. She'd been trying every number she had for Maggie and Nick and they weren't answering. Most likely they were all still asleep. Although Maggie had been known to shut off the main landline when the kids were sick, she usually left her cell phone on.

Riley had managed to buy Ally a ticket on the flight March had booked them on to Rome. When they reached their departure gate, Ally collapsed onto a seat, but Riley remained standing, watching, guarding. Always on high alert. He turned toward Kate. "Maggie's still not answering?"

"No." Kate ran a hand through her tangled hair.

She'd already talked to Shannon and warned her, so at least Shannon's family was safe. But it was going to take Shannon, Craig and the kids close to an hour to drive to Maggie's house in Bethesda. "I'm not getting on that plane until I get hold of Maggie."

"Understood."

She paced back and forth while waiting to board. "I need to walk."

"Stay where I can see you," he whispered.

Feeling testy, she glared at him. Who did he think he was bossing her around? *Oh, yeah.* A man whose sister-in-law was being held hostage. Kate had to admit she'd been wrong about Jenny. "For what it's worth," she whispered, "you have a very brave sister-in-law."

He glanced away. "I owe her more than you can imagine."

Kate doubted that, having been raised by two older sisters after their mother passed away, but for once she wasn't going to argue with him. Walking down the concourse, she glanced at her watch and dialed again.

Wake up, Mags. Wake up.

"Hello?" Maggie's voice, thick and slow, sounded over the line.

"Oh, Maggie, thank God you finally answered."

"Kate? It's so early. Are you all right?"

"I'm fine. Is Tessie okay?"

"Tessie? Well, she's got a cold, but it's not that big of a deal. Why? What's up?"

Kate felt near tears with relief. Riley was right. Her niece had missed school because she was sick. She glanced over, found Riley watching her, and nodded. *They're okay.*

His shoulders rose with a deep breath and he looked away, clearly relieved. Suddenly she couldn't believe she'd thought him in with March on this whole mess. She might not see eye to eye with him on much—well, not on anything, really—but none of his actions had ever indicated anything other than an upstanding moral character. In fact, now that she thought about it, he'd been rather uptight in that regard.

"Can I talk to Nick?" she asked Maggie.

"He's still dead to the world sleeping," she whispered. "We were awake most of the night with sick kids."

"Mags, it's really important."

"All right. Hold on."

Kate could hear Maggie rustling the bed covers and then muffled voices.

"Hey, Kate," Nick said a little groggily.

"Nick, I need you to do something."

"Name it." His voice turned instantly alert.

"Shannon and Craig are already on the way to your house. As soon as they get there, leave. Take everyone and go someplace safe. Make sure you're not followed."

There was a short pause on the line. "This have anything to do with the two guys I noticed watching the house all day yesterday?"

"So they are there." She'd been hoping March had been bluffing.

"I assumed they had something to do with the Kythos family mess I was involved in years back. As soon as I saw them, I called in a couple bodyguards for Maggie and the kids. But if this isn't Kythos family business, then what is it?"

"I don't have time to explain—"

"Don't worry about us. I can take care of Maggie and the kids." He could. Of that, Kate was sure. "I'll make sure Shannon and Craig are safe. But you need to tell me what's going on."

"It's nothing you can fix, Nick." But it was just like him to try.

"Are you safe? Maggie will never forgive me— I'll never forgive me, Kate—if something happens to you."

"I'm with Riley. Remember him from Greece?"

There was a short pause on the line. "You mean the bodyguard Angelo sent home with you?"

"Yes." They were boarding the plane. She had to go.

Wait a minute. Or did she? That's when it dawned on her. She could walk away from this entire mess. This wasn't her problem anymore. Nick could keep Maggie and Shannon safe along with Craig and the kids and her. All she had to do was join them. But what about Ally? And Riley? Big, tough, surly and burly man? Were *they* going to be all right?

"Do you trust him?" Nick asked.

Trusting men didn't come easily to Kate, never had, not with her father having walked out on their family before Kate had even been born. It hadn't helped that her mother had never dated after her divorce. Neither had either of her sisters, for that matter. They'd found their true loves right out of the starting gate. So trust? Riley?

Somehow he was different than most other men she'd known, but she couldn't put her finger on how. "I don't know, Nick."

"Kate, I'm coming to get you," Nick said. "Where are you?"

Riley was waiting for her by the gate, his expression unreadable.

"Kate?"

She needed a moment to think, to figure out what she should do. "I'll be home when it's over."

"When what's over? Where are you going—"

"I gotta go, Nick. I'll call in a couple days to explain. The plane's boarding."

"Kate—"

She clicked the cell phone off and looked up.

Riley was watching her as if reading the thoughts going through her mind. Slowly she walked toward him.

"Your niece?" he asked.

"She's safe. You were right. She stayed home sick from school yesterday. Nick noticed March's men watching their house yesterday, so he'd already called in some security."

"Smart man. Can your brother-in-law handle March's men?"

"Yes. They'll be all right."

She could walk away and wash her hands of this entire mess. But what about Jenny? What if March hurt her simply because Kate didn't go to Rome? Kate couldn't stomach the thought of March using her as an excuse to hurt Jenny. She glanced at Ally, recognized that stubborn, angry teenager, and she couldn't do it. Kate had never in her life turned her back on a problem. Right or wrong, she was a part of this.

"Good." He nodded. "Then you need to stay here in D.C. and get to your sister's house. This is no longer your battle."

"What? Wait a minute." She grabbed his arm. "That's my decision to make."

"Not really, no."

"But it's my fault March still has Jenny. She came looking for me. Besides, March is expecting me to check in with you in Rome."

A flash of uncertainty flickered in his gaze. "Jenny isn't your problem."

"I may not be related to her, but March will hold me responsible for her."

He knew she was right.

"Riley, like it or not, you're going to need my help."

His gaze sized her up one side and down the other. Though his assessment was primarily clinical, unemotional, there was a spark of something intense in his serious gaze that she couldn't name. It wasn't quite vulnerability, but it wasn't confidence either. It wasn't complete respect, but he wasn't dissing her.

"You ever fired a gun?" he asked.

"No."

"Know anything about explosives or security systems? Can you take out a two-hundred-pound man? Kick down a door? Ever driven a car at a hundred miles an hour?"

"No. I can't do any of that."

"Then what possible kind of help can you be?" He turned. "You'd be nothing more than a liability."

Talk about a brush-off. A really nasty one, and it bothered her. "Everything's black and white to you, isn't it?"

"Yep."

"Well, I got news for you. There are lots of

gray areas in life, and this is one of them. Just because I'm not a hotshot military lug doesn't mean I wouldn't be of some use. Who's going to take care of Ally?"

"She's my daughter. She'll be fine."

"What if you run into a replica, a fake like March was suggesting?"

"Then I'll deal with that when—if—it happens."

"So that's it? I'm kidnapped, held at gunpoint and it's over? Like that?"

"Would you rather I put a gun to your head and tell you to stay? Would that get through that thick skull of yours?"

"You don't need anyone, do you?"

"I sure don't need you."

"So that's what's bothering you, isn't it? That you might need a woman?"

"Doesn't have anything to do with you being a woman. I've fought practically side by side with a couple of good soldiers who happened to be women."

"Then what is it? That you might not be entirely self-sufficient?"

For an instant something akin to uncertainty flashed in his eyes. He wasn't sure. He knew he might need her, and the possibility obviously unsettled him. Ally, on the other hand, definitely did need her. "I'm going. Whether you want me along or not." Kate snatched a couple of boarding passes out of his hand as she brushed past him and went to the teenager's side. "It's time to get on the plane, honey. Let's go."

Clearly dragging, Ally stood and walked beside Kate until they reached the aircraft aisle. "Will you sit next to me?" she asked, frowning at her father. "I'm not sitting next to *him*."

"Sure." Kate followed Ally down the aisle and took the seat next to her. Riley's gaze skimmed over every single passenger, not once but twice, and the enormity of this situation sank in a bit deeper. This wasn't a game. Things could, probably would, go wrong. She might never see her sisters and their families again.

Even so, she couldn't seem to make herself leave the plane. Whether Riley wanted to admit it to himself or not, very soon the time would come when he was going to need her. If she had anything to say about it, he was going to say pretty please before she lifted a pinkie for him.

CHAPTER SIX

Tuesday, 12:30 p.m.

SIXTEEN PLUS HOURS of air time, two layovers, three screaming babies and no less than twelve arguments with Kate later, they arrived in Rome in the early afternoon, having lost an additional six hours as a result of time zone changes. There'd been no direct flights at such short notice, so they'd lost a day simply getting from point A to point B. The moment the plane landed, Riley checked his phone for messages and listened to one left by Trace.

"Yo, Riley. I found March as they were packing up and vacating the town house in D.C." Trace's matter-of-fact voice sounded clearly over voice mail. "Jenny's heavily guarded. They boarded a private plane, but I've got the flight plan. You were right. They're headed first to Tokyo. I've hired a jet and I'll be on my way by the time you get this message. I'm on it, man. Don't worry."

Don't worry. Maybe if the clock suddenly quit ticking.

He dialed March's cell number.

"March here."

"We just landed in Rome."

"Good. In the paperwork I gave you you'll find contact information for supplies you might need. Now let me talk to Kate."

Hesitating, Riley glanced at her.

"Riley?" March paused. "Put Kate on the phone."

"First let me talk to Jenny."

At the mention of Jenny, Ally leaned forward in her seat and watched him.

"That's not the way it works," March said. "I'll let you talk to Jenny *after* I've talked to Kate."

Lacking any other option, he handed the phone to Kate. He was still royally pissed that she'd completely disregarded his direct order and gotten on that plane back in D.C., but he was forced to, if not admire, at least appreciate the way she hadn't backed down. The average person, man or woman, would likely have run out of that airport the moment the realization hit that March was no longer a personal threat.

Kate put the phone to her ear. "What do you want?"

Riley couldn't hear March's response.

"Go to hell." She handed the phone back to Riley.

"Now Jenny," Riley said.

There were a few muffled sounds.

"James?"

"Jenny, are you all right?"

"I'm fine." In spite of everything, her voice sounded strong. "Is Ally okay?"

Riley glanced at his daughter. "Ally's good."

"Can I talk to her?" Ally quickly asked.

"There," March said, coming back on the line. "Now everyone's happy. Call me again once you've reached Athens." Then he disconnected the call.

Riley glanced at his daughter. "He hung up."

Ally's shoulders slumped.

"Is Jenny all right?" Kate asked as their plane taxied to the gate.

"For now." He glanced around her at Ally. "Trace is on Jenny's trail," he said, making sure to guard his words for Ally's sake. "He's got to catch up to March before he can figure out a way to get her safe, but he'll get Jenny back."

Ally had barely said more than ten words to Riley since they'd left D.C. Now her eyes watered as she glanced at him. "Are you sure, Dad?"

"As sure as I can be about anything."

Ally looked away from him to stare sullenly out the window.

The words to reassure her, comfort her, simply would not form in his brain. Give him any military objective and, with the appropriate equipment and manpower, chances were he'd successfully complete the mission. But kids? Completely perplexing.

Teenage girls were the worst, an outright mystery, one he had no intention of trying to solve.

The moment they'd filed off the plane, Ally stormed away from him. "Ally?" he called. "Where are you going?"

Naturally she ignored him.

"Ally!" He charged forward and grabbed her arm. "You need to stay close."

"Chill!" She yanked her arm away and rolled her eyes at him. "I'm just going to the bathroom!"

He shook his head as she disappeared into the restrooms. "Then why didn't you say that?" he mumbled to himself.

"Because that would make things too easy for you," Kate said, coming to stand by his side.

He debated letting her comment go, but a part of him wondered. "Too easy. How?"

"She's mad at you for leaving Jenny. She doesn't understand and she has no other recourse than to jerk you around."

"I did what I had to do. Jenny knows that." But it didn't stop him from feeling guilty. "I'm not going to try and explain myself, let alone make any excuses for my actions. It is what it is. Ally will have to deal."

"Whatever," Kate murmured. "It's your relationship."

"And you're such an expert?"

"No." She slowly shook her head. "Not even

close. But there is one thing I know for sure. You're lucky to have a daughter, Riley. A family. I wouldn't be so quick to turn your back on it all, if I were you."

"You don't know what you're talking about. I haven't turned my back on anyone." His defenses rose. What was taking Ally so long in the bathroom? "This conversation is over."

"Yes, sir."

"Let's get one thing straight." He glared at her. "If you're going to do this with me, you need to check the attitude."

"*My* attitude's not the problem."

"Last night you said you thought I had a problem with you. I think you've got a problem with me."

"Don't flatter yourself."

"Well, if it's not me, then what is it?"

She crossed her arms. "Pretty much all men."

"You don't like men. *That* explains it."

Refusing to take his bait, she looked away from him. They stood silently for a few more minutes before Ally came out of the restroom and immediately beelined toward a shop filled with books, magazines, souvenirs and snacks. "I want something to eat," she said over her shoulder.

"Ally, come on," Riley said. "We can get something to eat on the road."

"This'll take a minute. Chill!"

"I have a feeling she needs to be by herself for a bit."

He wanted to be in Ostia Antica before the church closed for the day, but they had time. He took a deep breath and mustered some patience. Kate stood quietly next to him, her arms crossed, glancing at the comings and goings of harried travelers. Another few quiet minutes passed before his curiosity got the better of him. "So what have you got against men anyway?"

She glanced at him as if gauging his sincerity.

"Honestly. I want to know."

"Nothing much," she said. "Except for the fact that my father walked out on my mom before I was born. I suppose a therapist might say that got the ball rolling."

"He never came back, never tried to touch base again?"

"No. And I've never gone looking for him, either. By all accounts we were far better off without him."

"No men in your life." He shook his head. "No wonder."

"I've had men in my life."

He said nothing, only held her gaze as if challenging her.

"Right out of high school, I interned with a master potter. Rufus Sherman. He was the nicest man I've ever known."

"Was?"

"Killed in a car accident several years ago. He taught me everything I know about art. And then some." She smiled, remembering him.

"Were you in love with him?"

"What?" She snapped her head toward Riley so fast it looked as if she might've strained a muscle.

He couldn't believe he was actually having this conversation with her, but at least it was keeping him from getting antsy while waiting for Ally. "Did you love Rufus?"

"God, no. He was very happily married. He and Elena celebrated their fortieth anniversary just before they both died."

"That doesn't answer my question," he said softly.

"No, I suppose it doesn't." She seemed to give it some thought. "No, I didn't love Rufus romantically, but in a lot of ways, I suppose, he was a role model. He was certainly the closest thing to a father I ever had."

"And he's very likely the man by which you measure all men."

"I suppose."

"Ever dated?" Riley asked.

"I'm twenty-seven." Kate glanced sideways at him. "What do you think?"

"And?"

"And nothing about any of those men changed my opinion about the male sex, in general. Apparently my sisters managed to nab the last good men on the planet."

"All two of them." He almost smiled.

"I know it sounds crazy," she said, sounding suddenly vulnerable, "but I look at Maggie and Shannon with their husbands and kids and their perfect homes and all I know is they're happier than I'll ever be."

"Ever? You've already given up on love? That's a bit cynical even for a tough character like you, isn't it?"

"I'll be thirty soon—"

"You mean in three years?"

"My point is I'm not as young as you think."

"Right." He shook his head. "So what's the first thing you look for in a guy?"

"He has to be smart."

"Oh, come on, be honest. You go for looks."

"Maybe. A little."

"So what kind of guy do you like to look at?"

"Slender. Not too tall," she said right off the bat. "Nice, clean-cut hair. No beards or mustaches. Tans and too many muscles say self-absorbed."

Again he almost smiled as he wondered what she considered to be too many muscles.

"And if he's got a cell phone growing out of his ear, I won't even look twice."

"You like suits?"

"As much as the next girl."

"College educated?"

"I see where this is going, and I am *not* an elitist."

"Maybe not. But I'll bet a man's appreciation for art is a must, right?"

"What's so wrong about understanding what I do?"

"Nothing, in and of itself. But you add soft-spoken, sensitive, good listener and funny to the mix and you've got a certain type of man. A *nice* guy."

"A guy like Rufus."

"Exactly. But *nice* isn't necessarily right for you."

"Thanks. Thanks a lot."

Now he'd hurt her feelings. *Good job, Riley.* What the heck was taking Ally so long? Unfortunately his curiosity got the better of him. Again. "Are you saying you've never fallen in love?"

"Nope."

That seemed ridiculous for a smart, beautiful woman her age. "How can that be?"

"A hazard of never getting past the third date, I suppose."

"You've never dated a man more than three times?"

"Never."

"How can you possibly get the measure of a man within three dates?"

"Easy. Date one doesn't usually count for much. Guys are usually putting a best foot forward. But I can sometimes pick up enough clues to know things won't be going anywhere. If we make it to the end of date two, the real man is starting to surface. By date three, he's there. If you pay attention."

"So you never give a guy a chance with date four, huh?"

"What's the point? I've dated enough to know. From my experience, there isn't a man out there worth his weight in packing peanuts. They're either insecure to the point of suffocating a woman to death or confident to the point of being arrogant. Overachievers or lazy. Obsessive organizers or slobs. And on the rare occasion when I've happened to find a man who seems to be a great match, he invariably finds something critically wrong with me."

"Like what?"

She looked away.

"Come on. Out with it."

"Well, apparently I do all kinds of things wrong."

"Like?"

"If it's not one thing, it's another. I've been asked if I could laugh more quietly, stop talking during movies, wear my hair shorter, longer, dress sexier, dress less sexy, learn how to cook, make the bed every once in a while, or, my personal favorite, express my opinion less forcefully, please?"

Her feelings had been hurt. The truth was there in her eyes. The words to reassure her formed in his mouth, but while he'd never been her date, he'd been one of those men in thinking her mouthy and obstinate.

"I've spent enough time pretending to be Goldilocks forever testing out men," she muttered. "The just-right man isn't out there."

Riley didn't buy it. There was someone for everyone. His someone had died. Hers was still out there. But this conversation had suddenly gotten way too personal for his tastes.

Thank goodness Ally came out of the store. Munching on a bag of chips, she fell into step with them. The girls were blessedly silent on their way to customs. Even so, Riley found himself studying Kate. She was cocky and stubborn. Then again, maybe she was simply rightfully confident. In any case, she unfortunately seemed to get sexier every minute he spent with her.

Shut it down, Riley. Right now. She's barely over twenty-five and you? Pushing forty, you old geezer. Besides, you can't have this woman in your life, no matter how sexy.

He and Kate were cut from the same cloth, too

much alike, and that was the makings for a disaster in any kind of relationship. Life was about balance. For every up there was a down, every right a wrong. Flip every cloud with a silver lining and you'd see its dark side. A hard man needed a soft woman. Unless that man had chosen to be a soldier, like him.

There was no such thing as balance in a soldier's life. Amy's death and Ally's birth had made him realize that soldiers had no right being in a relationship in the first place, let alone building families. No right whatsoever. And twenty years on active duty had confirmed that fact.

But you don't have to be a soldier anymore, a small voice whispered inside his head. If he signed those early-retirement papers he could make a new life for himself. He could do anything he wanted.

There was only one problem with that scenario. He didn't know how to start over, start fresh. Begin again. A man could never put his soldier's life completely in the past, so there was absolutely no point entertaining the concept. *Put it away.*

By the time Riley had finished his musings they'd made their way through customs. While he took care of renting a vehicle, Kate called Maggie. From what little he could hear of the one side of the conversation, Kate was making light of the situation, and he didn't blame her. If his family

had known the direness of some the missions he'd
completed through the years, they'd have had a
hard time sleeping at night. Sometimes ignorance
truly was bliss.

It was close to two o'clock by the time they made
their way outside. Rome was a lot warmer than
D.C. Although it was only about sixty degrees
outside, the clear, steady sun made it feel much
warmer.

"I think we should stop and get some sleep,"
Kate said, flipping on a pair of sunglasses.

Riley glanced at his daughter. Despite having
slept a good portion of their flights, she looked
jet-lagged. "We don't have time." As the bright,
hot midday sun beat down on his head, he climbed
behind the wheel of their rental car. "We need to
make contact with March's man first, then scope
out the church. After that, we'll find a place to stay
and get some sleep."

"But—"

"Kate." He glared at her. The woman had an
opinion on everything. "We have five days to steal
five statues in three different cities. Jenny doesn't
have time for us to screw around."

For a moment she considered him. "You're right.
I'm sorry." Her mouth snapped shut.

Well, I'll be damned. Apparently miracles did
happen. Without another word, Ally and Kate
climbed inside the car.

"First stop, March's contact," Riley said as he dialed the number March had included in the file he'd given them.

The call was answered immediately. *"Pronto,"* a man mumbled, speaking Italian.

"You have something for me," Riley said. "From March."

"Yes. Just before you get to Ostia there is a petrol station on the right. Pull in and wait."

Riley hung up, drove out of the airport and toward the coast.

"Where are we going?" Kate asked.

"A seaside town called Ostia Antica."

"At the mouth of the Tiber River."

He glanced at her. "You've been there?"

"No, but I know it's about thirty kilometers outside Rome. Shouldn't take us too long to get there."

"I want to scope out the church before it closes tonight."

"Too bad this isn't a vacation," Kate mused.

"I've practically never been out of D.C.," Ally grumbled as they zipped past the landscape.

"Well, Rome is a beautiful city. Filled with art. In fact, it almost *is* art."

"You've been to Italy before?" Ally asked.

"Four times." Kate smiled. "What about you, Riley?"

"Been to Rome several times."

"So you know what I'm talking about, then."

"Actually, no. I've only ever been here on assignment. Never had time to sightsee."

"For some reason, that doesn't really surprise me," Kate muttered.

Every foreign city he'd ever visited had been with the military, but he'd always had a job to do. He'd been to half the countries on the planet at one time or another. When hadn't he been either in the military or on military business?

"Someday you'll both have to come back and see the city properly. It's worth it."

"What's so great about it?" Ally asked, rubbernecking as they drove. "It doesn't look all that special."

"That's because we're out by the airport," Kate said. "This isn't the real Rome. The real Rome is spectacular. It's museums and ruins. Churches and chapels. The Vatican Museum alone houses the largest collection in the world of Leonardo da Vinci paintings. You can see the Pantheon, the Colosseum, the Spanish Steps. More fountains than you can shake a stick at and some of the best restaurants in the world."

"Pizza and pasta," Ally murmured.

"And seafood and wine. Cheeses and breads."

For the entire time it took to leave the city, Kate talked about one museum or ruin after another. In spite of everything on his mind, Riley caught himself listening and even enjoying her dissertation on the charms of Rome.

"It all sounds so beautiful," Ally murmured sleepily.

Riley glanced in the rearview mirror. Ally was lying down with her head propped against her pack. "She's asleep."

"Good."

"Thanks for…easing her mind," Riley whispered. He felt her eyes on him.

"Your daughter's a pretty neat kid."

"I know that."

"Do you?"

Riley glanced sideways at her. "What's that supposed to mean?"

"From what I've gathered, she doesn't even live with you."

For reasons he did not want to explore, this discussion with Kate seemed dangerous. "I've told you before. My personal life is none of your business."

"Maybe so, but—"

"Leave it. We're here." Riley pulled off the highway into the gas station and positioned the car with a clear view of the entire parking area and the ability to drive straight ahead if a quick getaway was necessary. He felt almost naked without a weapon.

"Now what?" Kate asked.

"You get into the driver's seat, and we wait."

"Why do you want me driving?"

Now more than ever he wished this woman had stayed in D.C. "Am I going to have to explain myself every step of the way?"

"How would you like following orders without question?"

What did she think he'd done in the military? But then, he had to admit, his trust and respect had not ever been given easily. He'd fought side by side with most of the men from whom he'd taken orders. Didn't Kate deserve the same opportunity, that he earn her respect before she unconditionally gave it?

He sighed and said, "Because if anything happens to me I want you ready to take off. Make sense?"

She nodded and switched places with him in the front seat.

Not more than a few minutes ticked by before a black sedan pulled into the parking spot next to them. The driver glanced at Riley.

"This is it," Riley whispered. "No matter what, stay in the car. The moment I get out, lock all the doors and open the trunk. If something happens to me, take off. No hesitation." He glanced at her. "Kate?"

"All right," she said.

Leaving the engine running, Riley got out of the car, glanced at Kate through the glass and pointed toward the locks. The instant he heard the tell-tale click, he moved to the rear of the vehicle. Without a word, the other man exited his vehicle and transferred a large black duffel bag into their trunk. Then the man got back into his car and drove away.

Riley glanced around, made sure no one was watching and unzipped the bag. Two semiautomatic handguns, some explosives material, ammunition, smoke bombs, a tool kit. Everything a man needed to rob a museum and kill a few guards. He hoped he wouldn't need half of it and would definitely have to leave everything here before catching their plane to Athens tomorrow morning, but better safe than sorry.

He was about to close the bag when he noticed a couple of empty boxes with plastic windows and Greek lettering. Riley picked one up. They looked like packaging for a kid's toy. Or a novelty gift. Like a statue. There was a note attached. "These should get the statues through customs." Apparently March had thought of just about everything.

Knowing him, there was probably a tracking device hidden in this mess, but for now Riley wasn't going to worry about that. Besides, March knew their game plan. Riley's only ace in the hole was Trace. He slipped a handgun out of the bag, slammed the trunk and climbed back into the car.

"Well?" Kate asked.

He checked out the gun's safety and clip, then stuffed it into his jacket pocket. Strange how being in possession of a gun made everything better. "Let's go steal those first two statues."

CHAPTER SEVEN

Ostia Antica was a dying coastal town barely worth a moment of attention as far as Riley was concerned. The sooner they found the church, the sooner he could steal the statue and the sooner they could head to Greece.

"This town is something," Kate said. "This was Rome's main port once upon a time."

"Ships couldn't travel up the river?" Ally asked.

"Not the big ones," Riley said. "Not back then."

The comment garnered raised eyebrows from Kate.

"I may not take in the sights, but that doesn't mean I have no culture."

"Right." Kate smiled. "So here in Ostia, more than two thousand years ago, merchandise from ships traveling the Mediterranean came here and was transferred to barges before heading to Rome."

Kate had picked up a tourist book, including maps and hours of main tourist attractions, the last time they'd stopped for gas. With Riley giving directions, she zipped through the town without incident. By the time they reached the church it was less than ten minutes before closing.

Kate pulled into the nearly empty parking lot and turned off the motor. "Okay, let's go."

"Oh, no," Riley said, grabbing the camera he'd purchased during their layover in the Amsterdam airport. "You two are staying here."

"Why?" Kate asked.

"I'm not staying out here in the car," Ally immediately added. "Like a dog."

He would've given them both his evil eye if he'd thought it might have made any difference, but it was quite clear neither of these two females was the slightest intimidated by him. How had that happened?

"Look," Riley said, spinning to the side so he could glare at both of them at once, "you two are staying in the car because I do not want either of you involved in this."

"There's no way around it, Riley," Kate said. "We're already involved."

"Yeah," Ally agreed. "And I'm sick of sitting. First the plane, then the car. I need to walk."

"Me, too."

"You two can walk all you want once I'm done here. We'll get some dinner and find a hotel. You'll be done with the car for the night."

"No," Kate said, opening her door. "I want to see the church."

"Me, too." Ally followed suit.

It was obvious these two had never served in the military. Some way, somehow he was going to have to impress upon them the meaning of a little thing called a chain of command, but just now he didn't have time.

"Fine. For now." He got out and snapped a few pictures of the exterior of the church. At least it was a few degrees cooler here than in Rome. "We're on vacation, okay? If anyone asks, we're a family."

Ally grinned at Riley. "But is Kate your wife or your daughter?"

Smart-ass.

"I'm too old to be his daughter," Kate said.

"Then that makes you my mom."

"But I'm not old enough for that."

"You'll do," Riley said. "Come on. Let's get this over and done with."

He crossed the parking lot and opened the front door to the church. Kate and Ally followed. They walked through the foyer—apparently there was no admittance fee—and went inside. Already the place was decorated for Christmas with lights and a nativity scene. An older couple, most likely Americans, walked around, reading displays, snapping photos.

He handed the camera to Kate. "You and Ally take some pictures. I'm going to walk around."

"Yes, sir." She mock saluted him.

Attitude. Again.

The old church smelled faintly of wood oil and incense, and a damp chill hung in the air. While Kate and Ally played tourist, Riley surreptitiously summed up the security, what little there was of it. If it hadn't been for the old couple, he might have considered walking out of there with the statues. Luckily, the building was at least several hundred years old and didn't appear to have been renovated to any great degree.

He found a collection of artifacts locked behind glass in a vestibule near the front of the church. The case didn't appear to be hooked up to any sensors. March was right. Chances were these people didn't yet know what they had on their hands. He studied the pieces on display. March had given him a general description, but all the statues looked the same to him.

"Relax," Kate whispered, sidling up next to him. "You look like you're on a mission, but you're supposed to be on vacation."

He turned toward her, suddenly curious. "Why are you doing this for me?"

"Who said I'm doing this for you? Maybe it's for Ally."

"Ally. That makes sense." He should have known.

It couldn't have anything to do with him. "So do you know which statues are the right ones?" he asked.

"Yes."

He waited a moment. "You going to tell me or what?"

"Not until you say please." She grinned up at him.

"What?"

"You heard me. Pretty please would be even better."

Clenching his jaw, he held back the tirade forming, although there was a part of him that wanted to smile.

"Admit that you need me, Riley, and then I'll tell you."

He'd never *needed* anyone except other soldiers his entire adult life. He took in her self-satisfied expression, the smart curl in her lips. Suddenly he wasn't sure what he wanted more—to wring her neck or kiss her. Probably both. Although kissing her was making headway. "Kate, this isn't a game."

"I'm waiting."

"Oh, for—fine. I need you! Okay?" In more ways than one, he was beginning to think.

"That wasn't so hard, was it?" Her eyes sparkled with mischief. "One is on the middle shelf, second statue from the left. That's Hemera. Goddess of daylight."

He located the piece, staring at it as he stood in front of the display case. "That one right there?"

"Yep."

Naked but for a swath of fabric covering her groin area, she was a very young-looking woman. Her hair was covered in some kind of crown of leaves and her breasts were small but perky.

"The other one," Kate whispered. "Nyx, goddess of night, is on the bottom, last one on the right."

Nyx was everything her daughter wasn't. While she might have been clothed, with only one full and lush breast exposed, the look on her face was anything but innocent.

This was going to be a long week.

"You're sure?" he asked.

"Positive."

Apparently, obstinate and opinionated came in handy every once in a while.

"And March is right," she continued. "They both have the signature rosebuds. See? In Hemera's hair? And on Nyx's shoulder, where her robe is clasped together?"

He nodded.

"When are you going to steal them?" she asked.

"Tonight. After the town closes down." He turned toward the front door, his prepaid cell phone rang, and the lightheartedness of the moment dissipated in an instant. There was only one person who'd be calling him on this phone. He snapped it open. "Trace?"

"Yeah, it's me."

Thank God. "Do you have Jenny?" he asked, stepping outside.

Kate followed him, her expression full of concern.

"No. But I caught up with them. Landed in Tokyo right on March's heels a few hours ago. March and two of his men took off, but Jenny's still on the plane. Still heavily guarded. I won't be able to get near her on my own."

Feeling frustrated and helpless, Riley turned away from Kate and hoped Ally stayed inside the church for another few minutes. He didn't know how he was going to tell her Jenny still wasn't safe. "Trace, you're going to need help."

"One step ahead of you, buddy. Already called in a couple favors. March's next stop is Shanghai. They're meeting me there."

"Is there anything I can do from my end?"

"No."

"Stick with her, Trace."

"Will do. I'll call you when I have something to say."

Riley hung up and glanced at Kate.

"You don't need to explain. I heard."

Ally came out of the church. "I'm starving."

"Me, too," Riley said, hoping he might evade updating Ally on Jenny. He held Kate's gaze, willing her to understand.

"Well, then, let's get something to eat," Kate said, forcing a smile.

Riley felt himself relax. "Then we can find a store for a few supplies, a hotel and get some sleep."

"I'M NOT LETTING YOU or Ally out of my sight," Riley said, glancing at Kate. "So we're all staying in the same room. Got a problem with that?"

"No." But she did have a problem with the accommodations. The main—nice—hotels in town were completely booked for the night due to a wine tasting sponsored by several local businesses, so they'd been relegated to an off-the-beaten-path dive.

The fact that the hotel was minutes from the old church didn't make up for the fact that it appeared to be a flea-bitten hole-in-the-wall. The carpets were threadbare, the hallway stank and a sign at the front desk warned all guests that the hot water would be turned off from midnight to 8:00 a.m. If the rooms weren't in any better shape, they were in for a real treat.

Apparently they'd used up their day's quota of luck on the fabulous trattoria they'd found a few blocks from the church. Riley had practically inhaled his order of spaghetti with clams. Kate's cappelletti romagnoli, ravioli in Bolognese sauce with butter and sage, was divine. And even Ally, apparently a relatively picky eater, had enjoyed her shrimp scampi risotto.

Riley opened the door to the triple room he'd rented and led the way inside, making sure there was no one in the bathroom or closet. "We're clear," he announced, throwing his jacket onto the bed closest to the door.

Kate glanced at the paint peeling off the walls and opened her mouth to protest, but Ally beat her to the punch.

"I am *not* sleeping here," Ally announced on examining the bed linens, which appeared to be dusty from disuse.

"If you're tired enough, you'll sleep." Riley glanced from Ally to Kate. With a couple days' growth of beard stubble on his face, he looked much sexier than he should have, but tired. "You got anything you want to add?"

Kate bit her tongue and shook her head. She'd given Riley enough of a headache for the day. "I'll deal. But I'm drawing the line if there are mice in the bathroom."

While Ally proceeded to pout, sitting on one corner of her bed with her arms folded petulantly, Riley went through what was clearly his hotel routine. He locked the door, then went to the sliding glass door, glanced outside and tested the lock. Next he took out his gun, checked the ammunition and safety and set it on the bedside table.

In the meantime, Ally had slowly sunk sideways onto the bed, her head barely managing to hit the pillow. Moments later, she was sound asleep.

Poor baby. Ally was trying so hard to hold it all together, but inside she was no doubt more frightened than she'd ever been in her life. She was much older and bigger than Kate's nieces and nephews, but she was still so much a child. Kate walked over to the bed and untied Ally's tennis shoes. Then she grabbed the blanket and laid it over Ally's prone form. When she glanced up, Riley was watching her.

"Thank you," he whispered. "I don't think of those things."

She shrugged.

"Will you be all right alone out here?" he asked softly. "I'd like to take a quick shower."

His concern for her welfare suddenly seemed touching rather than irritating. He might put himself out as gruff and callous, but she had a feeling that was anything but the truth. "You're not expecting anyone to bother us, are you?"

"Not really, but you never know."

"Go for it," she whispered back. "We'll be fine.

I'd like to take a shower, too, but you'll likely be done before I'm ready to go."

"You know how to use a gun?"

She glanced at the weapon on the table. "No."

He handed it to her, his fingers brushing lightly against her palm.

"Safety off. Safety on." He flicked a metal switch. "Aim. Pull the trigger. Steady your arm with a hand under the gun." He took her left hand and placed it under her right. "Got it? Otherwise the chamber action will cut you."

"Got it." The gun felt much heavier and his hands much warmer than she'd expected.

"You ever have to use this, Kate, don't try anything fancy. Hit your target. Anywhere. Okay?"

"Okay."

He held her gaze for a long moment, looking as if he might try to convince her to head back to the States.

"Don't even bring it up again, Riley," she said, cutting him off before he could open his mouth. "I'm here because I want to be here, and I'm seeing this through. When it's all over, you're going to be glad I did."

Without a word, he turned and went into the bathroom. A second later, the spray of the shower sounded. Appreciative of the fact that Riley had thought to stop after dinner and buy each of them a backpack, some toiletries and a few changes of clothing, Kate dug through her bag.

By the time she'd gathered her supplies and some clean clothes, he'd finished in the shower. He came out of the bathroom wearing sweatpants but bare chested, with droplets of water still clinging to the side of his arm. For a moment she stared. Couldn't help herself. Well built didn't begin to describe Riley without a shirt. His arms looked chiseled from rock. A dusting of dark curly hair was scattered across his muscular chest.

What she would have done at that moment for a hunk of clay to sculpt and mold and attempt to do justice to this man's perfect body. Then again, she wasn't sure that was even possible.

"All yours." He held open the door, looking down at her.

Him or the bathroom?

"The shower's nothing fancy," he said quietly. "But it does the job."

Their hotel room was narrow and small, requiring her to get far too close to him to make her way into the even tinier bathroom. If the heat in his gaze was any indication, he, too, was affected by their proximity. Was it her imagination wanting him to, or had he actually moved closer to her?

Feeling breathless, she reached out to steady herself and her hands flattened against him. Riley's bare chest felt wonderful. Thick springy hair and soft, warm, velvety skin over tense, hard muscles. Oh, and he smelled so good, clean soap, heat and something so male she could almost taste him. What *would* he taste like?

His head tilted down toward her, her head tilted back and as if in a dream, their lips touched. A low sound vibrated from his throat as he deepened the kiss, causing the stubble on his cheeks to graze her soft skin. Then his tongue slipped through her teeth and she leaned into him, virtually melting against him.

His arms went quickly around her, holding her up, holding her to him. For an instant, like a rag doll, she was his to bend, to mold, to take, but then they both seemed to come to their senses at the same time. She stiffened. He released her, stepped back and glanced at Ally, as if only then remembering she was in the room.

Kate sucked in a breath. *That did not just happen. That could not have… Oh, yes, it did.* As sure as she was standing there, her cheek felt tender from where his whiskers had rubbed against her skin.

Mortified, she rushed into the bathroom, quickly closed the door and leaned back against it. She could still feel the warmth of his hands on her back, his lips on her mouth, and God help her but it took every ounce of her willpower not to open the door and finish what they'd started.

CHAPTER EIGHT

THE LOCK TURNED IN the bathroom door and Riley stood there for a moment, thinking maybe he'd imagined that kiss. No such luck. The lingering velvety pressure of her lips on his mouth and the tightening in his groin proved it had been far too real. How could he have let that happen?

She'd put her hands on his chest, a gesture in and of itself not that forward, but couple it with the look of longing in her eyes and all he'd been able to think about was having her hands all over him, his all over her.

Putting his lapse in judgment down to jet lag and lack of sleep finally catching up to him, he took a deep breath to clear his thoughts and pulled a T-shirt over his head. Then he checked on Ally. Down for the count. With any luck, he would be, too, within a few minutes.

He spread out on one of the other beds and closed his eyes, hoping the sound of the water spraying in the shower would lull him into oblivion. Instead, his brain immediately went to work imagining bare, wet, female skin. Kate naked in a shower. Wouldn't that be a sight for tired eyes?

The remembered image of her as a teenager in only a bra and thong popped into his mind. Her tattoos. The lines of her curves. He couldn't help but wonder how she'd matured. Probably to absolute perfection.

He tossed and turned a few more times. Finally accepting there was no chance he'd be falling asleep any time soon, he swung his legs out of bed, slid open the balcony door and sat near the rail. A relatively warm autumn breeze blew in from the Mediterranean. He took his mind off the sound of the shower stopping by locating the church and studying its dark outline. Although the nearest streetlight was half a block away and there were no lights either inside or outside the building, a nearly full moon illuminated the sky, destroying any cover the night would provide. That wasn't good.

The bathroom door opened behind him and the sheets rustled as Kate climbed into bed. With his luck, she was in some skimpy tank top and shorts and he'd get a good eyeful in the morning. The sheets and pillow rustled a little more as she seemed to be getting comfortable. Then the room was quiet.

This is great. He could look forward to several more days—and nights—of close quarters with Kate. *You were too old for her ten years ago. You're still too old.*

Soon there were more sounds of movement. Quiet footsteps.

Do not come out here. Please, do not—

"Can I join you?" Her voice came from the sliding door.

He shifted, took in the sight of her shiny, clean face, dark, wet hair and thanked his lucky stars that the T-shirt she'd bought to sleep in was at least an entire size too big for her. Add a pair of baggy sweats to the picture and there should've been nothing to stimulate his imagination. That was, until he found himself wondering what lay beneath all that excess fabric. But that wasn't her fault.

"Sure," he said quietly, hoping to avoid any discussion about the kiss.

She sat in the other chair, a rusting, wobbly hunk of metal similar to the one he was sitting in, and looked out at the twinkling lights of the old city. The moon shining over the ocean. "It might be a crappy hotel, but the view is spectacular."

He said nothing. Small talk was okay. No talk would be better. Especially once he caught sight of those tiny blue butterflies on her wrist and his mind immediately tracked to the ones on her side.

"Look," she said, swallowing, "what happened earlier—"

"Nothing happened earlier." Reaching behind him, he pushed the sliding door closed so their conversation wouldn't wake Ally.

"That's funny, because I thought we kissed."

Silently he looked up into the sky.

"It's my fault," she whispered. "All those years ago. When you escorted me home from Greece. You were the first grown man... Well...I've always wondered... Let's say I had quite a crush on you."

Say what? He wasn't the kind of guy women developed crushes over. "Like I said. Nothing happened."

"That's the way you want to play it?"

"You got it."

Her sigh was soft, impatient. "Okay. Fine. It never happened."

For a while she sat silently glancing out toward the ocean. He was beginning to think he was going to get away without any deep conversation when she opened her mouth again. "What was she like?" she asked. "Your wife."

He did not want to go there. Not now. Not ever. And definitely not with Kate.

"Tell me about her. What did she look like? Was she similar to Ally? Or to Jenny?"

It had been more than ten years since Amy had died, and Riley could still conjure her image in his mind in less time than it took his heart to beat.

"She looked like an angel," he said before thinking better of it. "Clear blue eyes. Long blond hair, like Ally's, only curly. Yes, she and Jenny were very similar."

He felt his expression soften at the memory of his wife. "Amy was the sweetest woman I've ever known. Never raised her voice. Never swore. Always had a kind word on the tip of her tongue. That woman stuck her neck out anytime for anyone, but she was soft-spoken about it. I don't think we ever once got into a fight."

She'd been Riley's complete opposite. As kind, generous and forgiving as he was stoic, judgmental and harsh.

"It must've been hard to lose her," Kate whispered. "How did she die?"

He considered shutting her out as he had back in D.C., but there no longer seemed to be a point. "Amy had something called rheumatic heart disease. For the most part, she was pretty healthy. You never would've known she was sick."

"Is that something she was born with?" Kate curled her legs underneath her, as if settling in.

"No. The doctors thought an untreated case of strep throat from when she was about twelve, only a little younger than Ally, damaged her heart valves. It had some impact on her life going forward, but it wasn't crippling. She couldn't play basketball or soccer, that kind of thing, but she didn't care about any of that. For her, the worst thing was knowing she should never have children."

"Why not?"

"Pregnancy puts a lot of strain on the heart. Too much for her condition."

"Did you know she had this disease?"

"Not right away, no. Her family was pretty quiet about it. Then we started dating in high school. Got pretty serious, I thought, but every time I tried talking about a future together, she'd clam up. She knew I'd always wanted to be a soldier, so I figured she didn't want to be a military wife."

He sighed, the memories flooding his senses. "About the time I started getting ready to head off into the marines her dad pulled me aside and made her health situation crystal clear. If Amy got pregnant, most likely either she or the baby would die, probably both." He swallowed and looked away.

"Scared you, didn't he?" she whispered.

"I imagine that was his intention. He knew I cared for Amy, but he wanted to make sure we didn't do anything stupid before I went off to boot camp."

"So you never…"

"No. There was no way I was going to take the chance of getting her pregnant," he said, lowering his head. "But by the time I came home on my third or fourth leave…well, let's just say I wasn't a virgin of much of anything anymore."

"Did you tell her?"

He nodded. "We had long talks. About our future. Her health. I was fine with not having kids, but not having sex…wasn't going to happen. I loved her. I asked her to marry me, got fixed and three months later we were husband and wife."

"How did she get pregnant?"

"I went in for all the scheduled tests, thought I was shooting blanks, but apparently my vasectomy didn't take."

"But the doctors would've told you."

"They told Amy."

Her gaze turned quizzical. "And she didn't tell you?"

"I'd just left on a mission when the lab called with the test results. I was gone three months. She had a lot of time to think and things changed for her. At least, that's what she told me after we found out she was pregnant. She started believing the possibility of having a child was worth the risks of pregnancy." He paused. "So she didn't tell me we were risking her life every time we made love."

"It wasn't your fault."

"Sure it was. There were signs. I should've seen them. Besides, I made love to her. My baby. My fault."

"That's harsh."

"Not as harsh as what she had to deal with afterward." He shook his head. "The doctors recommended she terminate the pregnancy. It was the only way to guarantee she'd live." He took a deep breath. "She refused."

Riley completely understood, accepted and respected Amy's death-sentence decision. Put in the same position, it was exactly what he would've done, but that didn't make the consequences any easier to live with. "What is it with women and kids, anyway?" he said, shaking his head.

Warily she glanced at him. "The desire for family to nurture and love is pretty strong in a lot of women."

"Even in you?"

She sat a little straighter. "What's that supposed to mean?"

"You don't seem...generally speaking...like the mothering type."

Her amber eyes flashed with moonlight and irritation. "So strong-willed, independent women can't have families, is that it?"

"That's not what I meant."

"I could be as good a mom as any other woman."

Obviously he'd hit a nerve. "I'm sure you could," he said, hoping to drop the conversation.

"So then what did you mean by the comment?"

Oh, hell. He truly couldn't picture this tough cookie as a mother, and there was no doubt that if he kept talking he'd keep digging his hole deeper and deeper.

"I'm waiting," she said, with no intention of letting him off the hook.

"I meant…only that you seem more balanced," he said slowly. "As if you understand that there's more to life. That's all."

"Is there more to life?" Kate studied him. "Maybe you hadn't given much thought to kids. Maybe you didn't want them at all. But when you first looked into Ally's little face, how did you feel then?"

Like the scum of the earth. It was, after all, his fault Amy had gotten pregnant. His fault that Ally's mother had died. He'd done his best to be a good husband, but he'd barely gotten the chance. And being a single father? Wasn't in the cards.

"The first time I looked into Ally's eyes," he said, "I felt…humbled. Completely out of my league. A baby. What was I supposed to do with a baby? Kids were Amy's forte.

"I remember sitting in the dark in the hospital room, right before she gave birth to Ally. The last thing she said to me was 'I want to see her face. Just once.' She never got the chance." Riley's throat tightened with emotion. "Ally was six weeks premature," he whispered. "Amy died during the delivery."

The helplessness he'd felt back then enveloped

him. Every day, Amy worsened. Every day, she was one day closer to death. There was no weapon in the world that could fight off that particular threat, no armor heavy-duty enough to protect the sweetest woman he'd ever known. All of Riley's military training had been worthless. In the end, there hadn't been a thing he could do to save her. Proving to him once and for all that a soldier had no business falling in love and making families. No business raising children.

"All my training, all those years of holding lives in the balance, and I couldn't do a thing to save my own wife."

"You're a soldier, Riley, not God."

"Doesn't matter. I knew right then and there…" He paused. "I had no right being a father."

"So that's why Jenny's been raising Ally?"

Riley nodded. "Ally hadn't been out of the hospital a week before she got sick and ended up back in intensive care." He stared out at the lights of Ostia Antica. "Jenny was single, unmarried and distraught over Amy's death. And she was about as attached to Ally as an aunt could be. Spent every day at the hospital."

Leaving Ally in his sister-in-law's care had seemed like the right answer for everyone concerned. Jenny would have a baby in her life, and Riley was able to go back into the military where he belonged without having to worry about messing up in caring for an infant.

"That had to be hard for Ally," Kate said. "Growing up without her mother or father."

Riley glanced at her. "She was better off with Jenny."

"I'm sure that's what you've had to tell yourself."

His defenses rose. "Hold on there."

"You grew up with your parents, right? And they're both still alive?"

"Yeah," he said cautiously.

"Well, I grew up without either of mine. Not having a dad was hard, but manageable. My mom dying when I was eight tore me apart. I can't tell you what I would've given as a kid for a complete family." Quiet for a moment, she glanced at her wrist.

"The tatt. It's for your mom, isn't it?"

"Yeah," she whispered. "Maggie got one first. Shannon was next. Then me. We all have different colors and designs, but we all chose butterflies. Mom loved them. Moths, too. She even hatched a cecropia from a cocoon one year."

"One of those big, brown prehistoric-looking things?"

"Yeah. It was amazing. One of my last memories of her is of an afternoon she spent with us three girls at the park picnicking and chasing butterflies with a net." She paused, as if reliving the memory. "Maggie did the best she could for being only sixteen when my mother died, but barely a day went by that I didn't wish for Mom back in my life. For a full and complete family. For all of us to be together again. I missed her so much." She glanced at Riley. "I'm sure Jenny does her best, but no one can love Ally the way you can."

"Ally knows I love her."

"You sure about that?"

Riley said nothing. What could he say? With the way Ally had been acting toward him lately, Kate could be right.

"I'm sorry," Kate whispered. "That you lost Amy."

"Nothing for you to be sorry about. Wasn't your fault. Anyway, life goes on."

"Seems like it didn't for you," she whispered. "You might've carried on with your military career, but you lost your connection with your daughter."

"I'm a soldier. It's my life. My choice." He sighed, thinking again of those retirement papers. If he signed them, what would he do with himself? He didn't know how to be anything but what he was. "I had no business being married in the first place. No business having a child. Things worked out, in the end, the way they needed to be."

"How can you say that? You have a daughter. You shouldn't turn your back on her."

He'd never turned his back on anyone in his life. He'd simply accepted his limitations where Ally was concerned. "Jenny's been the best thing for Ally." And with that, he'd better get his ass off to bed before he did something really, really stupid. Like kiss Kate again or worse. He pushed back his chair, suddenly exhausted. Now he could sleep.

"About that kiss—"

"What kiss?" He stood and walked toward the sliding door.

Riley had been with plenty of women since Amy had died, but not one of them had been the kind looking for a relationship. Fly-by-night, no ties let alone commitments had been all he'd been interested in. Kate had made it crystal clear tonight that she wasn't that kind of woman. Not by half. She'd expect nothing less than everything—a home, family, the whole shebang—from a man, and she'd deserve it, too. A big fat nothing was all Riley had to offer.

"You want a family, Kate. But I'm not a family man. Been there. Done that. Will never do it again."

CHAPTER NINE

Wednesday, 4:30 a.m.

"KATE, WAKE UP."

The voice, soft but commanding, seemed a great distance away.

"Kate, we have to go."

"No," she whispered, snuggling deeper into the pillow. "Must sleep."

"Must steal the statues," the deep voice said. "Then sleep."

Riley.

She sat up, blinked and cleared the sleepy fog from her brain. Since she'd never been a morning person, it was not an easy thing to do. The room was illuminated with moonlight. She glanced at the clock. "You said we were leaving in the morning."

"It is morning."

"Maybe in boot camp."

Riley was dressed completely in black, and she could barely make out his shape as he moved to the other bed.

"Time to move, Ally," he whispered.

She moaned.

"Let's go."

"I'm tired," she murmured. "Come back and get me when you're done."

"Don't have the time for that. We need to hit the road as soon as I've got the statues. Come on, Al. This is for Jenny, remember?"

At that Ally opened her eyes, sat up and dropped her feet onto the floor. In two minutes flat they were all heading out to the car. Riley threw their packs into the trunk and drove without headlights toward the church. He pulled off on a side street facing the rear of the church, parked and immediately shut off the engine.

Kate glanced into the backseat at the same time as Riley. Ally looked as if she'd fallen asleep again.

"I'm going in alone," he whispered, clearly trying not to awaken his daughter. "I want you to stay out here with Ally."

"But—"

"No buts, Kate." He held her gaze. "Any number of things could go wrong in there, and you've done what I've needed you to do inside the church. You've identified the statues. The most helpful place for you right now is keeping an eye on Ally."

She knew he was right, but it still didn't sit well.

"Kate, I don't have time to argue."

"Then don't," she whispered. "Go. And be careful."

He'd opened his car door when a thought occurred to her. "Riley? Maybe I should have a gun."

"No." He gave a short and brisk shake of his head. "I don't want you pointing a weapon at anyone, because I don't want anyone else pointing one at you or Ally. This will take me fifteen minutes. Tops. If you hear police sirens, you drive away. Immediately. And you don't look back. Understand?"

Like that was going to happen.

"Kate."

"All right, fine," she said, pretending to go along with him.

He held her gaze for a long, still moment as if he knew what was going through her mind but also knew there was no point in continuing to argue. With a final glance back at Ally, he left the car, disappearing into the shadows along the street. The first few minutes ticked by slowly. Other than one car passing by two blocks ahead on the main thoroughfare, nothing moved.

Bored and fidgety, Kate flipped down the mirror, smoothed her hair and pulled it into a ponytail. Out of nowhere, her conversation with Riley on the hotel balcony started eating at her. His wife's death had thrown him for more of a loop than he was willing to admit, probably even to himself.

The sweetest woman he'd ever known.

So why had he kissed Kate? Why had that moment last night as they were passing each other at the bathroom door turned hot and bothered in the blink of an eye?

Nothing had happened. Right.

She studied her reflection in the mirror and tried to imagine what Riley saw when he looked at her. She was pretty, she supposed, but not beautiful. Not a blue-eyed blonde with curly hair. She wasn't half as pretty as Jenny, or most likely Amy. And she certainly was not angelic. More like a dark-haired devil. A mouthy, mulish, outspoken shrew.

No. That's not who she was. She was intelligent, strong willed and independent. She didn't have it in her to be anything or anyone else. And if that meant there was no man who could love her as she was, so be it. She refused to lose herself for any man. She refused to settle. Ever.

You want a family, Kate....

She wasn't likely to find one with James Riley. She didn't need three dates to figure that out. That meant forgetting the kiss they'd shared last night had ever happened.

Flipping the mirror closed, she studied the streets. The five minutes Riley had been gone turned into ten. The only sound inside the car was

Ally's soft, steady breathing. When ten minutes turned to fifteen, Kate's heart started pounding in her ears, her mouth turned dry and she couldn't seem to swallow.

What was taking him so long?

A sniffle sounded from the backseat. Kate glanced behind her and found Ally wide-awake, trying hard not to cry.

"What if he doesn't come back?" Ally whispered.

"He'll be back."

"But what if something happens? What if… he gets shot or arrested? Would you really leave him?"

"Absolutely not," Kate whispered.

"But you told him—"

"I told him what he needed to hear to get this done and over with. But I won't be turning my back on your dad, Ally. No matter what he tells me to do."

"Thank you."

For all her teenage blustering to the contrary, Ally clearly loved her father. "He loves you, you know?"

"Then why…why does he leave me with Jenny?" Instead of anger in her voice, Ally sounded hurt and alone.

"I'm going to guess it's because the idea of being

a father scares your dad more than the thought of going to war."

"Maybe if I was...easier. Nicer." Ally slid down in the seat, resting her head against her pack. "Maybe he'd stay."

"Ally, don't say that. It's not your fault. He's just...he's—"

"So stupid sometimes."

She could say that again. "You miss him, don't you?"

"I want him...home."

Kate understood. Completely.

When she glanced back again, Ally's eyes had drifted closed. The urge to climb into the backseat and hold the scared girl nearly overwhelmed Kate. Riley really was an idiot.

Headlights appeared and she jumped as a car turned onto their street and drove by them. An instant later the passenger door opened and Kate nearly had a heart attack until she saw Riley's face. "I didn't even see you coming," she whispered.

"It's my job to disappear. I've gotten pretty good at it." He checked on Ally, then handed the statues to Kate. "Did I grab the right ones?"

"Yes."

"Are they real?"

One at a time she flipped them upside down and around and turned them over and over in her hand.

"The weight feels right, but I need some light to get a better look."

Riley turned on a small but powerful flashlight and shone the beam directly onto the statues.

There was a nice-size chip in the lower side of one, but with the age of these pieces, if anything, that was an indication it was authentic. The tooling seemed rough, fitting the period, and the rosebuds, fully bloomed but small, were consistent with what she knew of the other statues. "I think they're real."

"Is there any way to be sure?"

"Not without carbon-dating them."

"All right, then. Like March said. Piece of cake." Riley took out the empty boxes March had prepared and slid the statues inside. They fit perfectly within the molded plastic sheathing. "That should work. Now let's get back to the airport. We have to catch a flight to Athens."

They switched places so Riley could drive. He shifted the vehicle into neutral and let it coast most of the way down the hill before starting the engine. Keeping the headlights off, they disappeared into the night.

"Two down," she whispered.

"Three to go." He glanced at her. "Thank you, Kate. I couldn't have done that without you."

That's when it happened. He smiled. It was the first smile Kate had ever seen on Riley's face and, given the flutter of pleasure rippling through her, she hoped it wouldn't be the last. Then again, she'd be a lot safer if he stayed pissed off the rest of the week.

RILEY PACED THE HALLWAY at the Rome airport as they waited to board their flight to Athens, keeping the restroom door in sight and wishing Kate would hurry it up. Ally was sitting nearby staring off into space while she listened to music from an MP3 player Kate had bought for her on the way to their departure gate.

Ally didn't look good. In fact, she looked stressed and tired and scared. Almost as if she was in shock. His instincts had him wanting to entirely ignore the situation. He'd rather take his chances with a cell of terrorists than a teenage girl, especially one as outspoken as Ally, but his conversation with Kate the night before reverberated through his mind in vivid sound bites.

What I would've given as a kid for a complete family...had to be hard for Ally growing up without her mother or father...you lost your connection with your daughter...shouldn't turn your back on her...no one can love Ally the way you can.

Was it possible Kate was right? At least in part? It may not have been his intention to turn away from his own daughter, but then Ally didn't know that, did she?

So quit turning your back. She's your daughter, man. Start acting like a dad and fix this.

He forced himself to walk toward her while keeping a clear view of the restrooms. "Ally?"

She glared up at him.

"How are you holding up?"

She rolled her eyes and removed one earpiece. "Why would you care?"

"Hey. I want to know how you're doing."

"Oh, I'm fine," she said sarcastically. "Kidnapped, held at gunpoint, my aunt could die and I'm watching you steal things. What could be better?"

Now that he thought about it, he supposed his question had been extremely lame. So how did an adult go about talking to a teenager in these extreme circumstances?

"Very funny." He sat, hoping he might be able to make some kind of connection with her over the music she was listening to. Within seconds it was apparent that wasn't going to happen. "Will you take those earpieces out for a minute?"

"Why?" Ally looked at him, her eyebrows raised.

"Do you need to be such an ass?"

"To you, yes."

"I'm trying to have a conversation with you."

"Want to get to know me? Find out who I am? Make a connection?"

"Yeah. What's so bad about that?"

"If I was three, nothing. But since you haven't been in my life for most of the last thirteen years, everything."

"Ally, listen—"

"No, you listen." She pulled out both ear-pieces. "You may be my father, but you are not my dad."

She was right. "I want to be. I want to try, anyway."

"How can you try when you don't know anything about me?" She stood and crossed her arms. "Tell me, *Dad*. What's my favorite color? What kind of grades do I get in school? Have I ever been kissed by a boy? Who's my best friend? Then again, do I even have any friends? Maybe I'm the nerd who gets bullied. Or the creepy Goth that scares everyone. You don't even know what kind of birthday cake I like."

He hesitated, knowing he should probably keep his mouth shut, but this one he knew. "Chocolate."

"Wrong," she said. "Jenny likes chocolate. Yellow cake is my favorite."

Holding eye contact with her at that moment was one of the hardest things Riley had ever done. "If you'll let me, Ally, I'd like to know the answers to all those questions. I've even got a few of my own."

She glared at him.

"In the last thirteen years a day hasn't gone by without me thinking about you," he said. "Wishing things had been different, wishing your mother had lived. Wishing…I'd stayed with you." As tough as it was for him to admit it, Kate had been right last night. "I should've raised you. But you have to know I did what I thought at the time was the best thing for you."

A voice came over the intercom announcing they were boarding their flight and Kate came walking toward them from the restroom.

"Best for me, or for you?"

"I screwed up. I'm sorry."

"That's supposed to make everything better?"

"No. But we need to start somewhere—"

"You mean *you* need to start." She grabbed her bag and stalked toward the flight attendants taking tickets. "I don't."

CHAPTER TEN

PARKED ON A SUNNY Athens hillside near the top of Mount Lykavitós, Kate sat in the driver's seat of their rented vehicle while Riley analyzed Angelo Bebel's estate through a pair of binoculars. Despite the fact that an uncharacteristically warm fall breeze blew through the open car windows, everyone in the car was irritable and antsy.

"Well?" Kate asked when she couldn't stand it any longer.

"All I can see is a guard at the gate and at least one more patrolling the exterior wall," Riley said. They were less than a quarter of a mile from their target, but the privacy of the grounds was protected by not only a six-foot concrete gate, but also a variety of bushy jacaranda, fig and laurel trees.

"It's what you can't see that's going to be the real problem," Kate said.

On the two-hour flight from Rome to Athens earlier that day, Riley had studied all the information March had passed on with regard to the state of Angelo's security. Curious, Kate had gone through everything with him. She'd been fascinated by his detailed knowledge of security systems. No wonder March had wanted him, so to speak, on his team.

"There's no doubt about it," Riley muttered, lowering the binoculars. "Angelo's security is as strong as it was ten years ago. A piece of cake this is not. Unless his people still haven't fixed that blind spot on the northwest corner of the grounds."

"Can I look?" Kate asked.

He handed her the binoculars. "I need to be finished with Moscow and on to Istanbul within a couple of days. I don't have time to stake out this place, let alone sit tight and wait for an opportunity to make a move."

"Why don't you just ask Angelo for the statue?"

"And if he says no? Then what?"

She lowered the binoculars. "Then he knows what you're after and he'll be on high alert."

"Exactly." He sighed. "Angelo might be a friend, but when money is involved—a lot of money—it's best to play it safe."

"My brother-in-law is very close with Angelo. He's like an uncle to him. Nick could ask."

"And if Angelo declines…"

"Again. He knows what you're after." Stealing it was their only option. "You can't just walk in there in the middle of the day."

"No. But I can wait until security lightens a bit.

Used to be Angelo had a standing date for Diloti on Wednesday nights."

"What's that?"

"A card game. He waits until Nadi goes to bed and then he meets a group of friends at a local tavern. He usually takes at least one security guard with him and plays late into the night. I need only a half hour, an hour tops. It'll be the best chance I've got to get inside undetected."

"What if he doesn't leave to play cards?"

"Then we wait until the house goes quiet."

Kate sighed. "So we wait either way."

"You got it."

"Here? In the car?" Kate asked. "All afternoon?"

Riley glanced back at Ally—who'd said barely a word since the airport and was watching them with a worried expression—before he turned to Kate. "We could all use a diversion."

Meaning Ally needed some downtime. "Good idea," Kate said, keeping it light. "I know just the place."

They arrived at a parking lot near the Acropolis, Athens's most famous ruins at the city's center, a short time later. Riley and Kate got out of the car, but Ally didn't budge.

Riley opened the back door. "Come on, let's go."

"I don't wanna." Ally pulled the door closed again, crossed her arms and turned away.

Clearly frustrated, he ran a hand over his face. "I'm so sick of putting her through this. It feels like this nightmare is never going to end."

"After tonight, there's only Moscow," Kate said, walking toward him. "Then it's almost over."

"I know. I wish we could get this done sooner rather than later."

"Let me talk to Ally," Kate said, putting her hand on his arm. It felt surprisingly natural to touch him. "I'll see what I can do."

He glanced into her eyes and was about to argue when it seemed he thought better of it. "I'll go get us some tickets," he said, walking away.

Thirteen. Kate wouldn't go back to that tumultuous age for a million bucks. She contemplated Ally as she sat with her back against the car door, her knees drawn toward her chest. She was hurting, but there was no way she was about to let anyone fix this for her, especially not her dad. Kate well remembered her own stubborn sense of independence, especially toward her sister Maggie, and the truth was that sometimes the teenagers who seemed the toughest were really the easiest to hurt.

Opening the back car door, Kate leaned inside. "Will you at least get out of the car and walk with me?"

"Go away," Ally said.

"I would, but see…there's this stubborn part of me that can never leave things be. You know?"

"Whatever."

"You and I have something in common, I've discovered."

"So you wanna be best friends?" She blew out a short burst of air. "I don't need any friends."

"My mom died when I was little. She got pancreatic cancer. I was only eight. So I think I understand a little of what you might be going through right now."

"You think, huh? Well, at least you knew your mom. My mom died when I was a baby. All I have are pictures, some videos. I don't remember her at all."

"Yeah, I suppose you have a point. I was lucky. I knew what I was missing. That made it easy."

Ally glanced at Kate and her face softened ever so slightly. "I'm sorry. I didn't mean it like that."

Kate gave a swift shake of her head. "It's okay. I'm going to guess some things about your mom dying are harder because you never knew her, and some things about my mom dying are harder because I did. But I think there are things about losing a mom that every child experiences."

A sullen silence followed, but at least it was better than nasty comments.

"It's got to be even scarier that your aunt, the

closest thing you've ever known to a mother, is in danger."

At that, several fat tears dropped off Ally's lashes and onto her cheeks.

"For what it's worth, I don't think they'll hurt Jenny."

"She could be dead already."

"I don't think so, Ally. David March needs your dad's help, and he knows the only way your dad will do what March wants is if Jenny is safe."

"You think?"

Kate nodded, wrapped an arm around Ally and squeezed her tight. "I know you're pretty mad at your dad. But he thinks he's doing what's best for you."

"He's wrong."

"Probably. But people, even parents, make mistakes."

"Does your dad ever make mistakes?"

"He made a big one. He left our family before I was born, so I never knew him."

"Really?"

Kate nodded.

"Do you miss him?"

"I don't think so. Maggie, my older sister, claims he was a real jerk. But I do miss having a dad. I miss having a family."

"You have sisters. You're lucky."

"Yeah, I am. And you have a dad who loves

you, even though he doesn't know how to show it. He'll do anything for you. And he'll do whatever it takes to make sure Jenny doesn't get hurt. He's pretty amazing, you know." And as she spoke those words, Kate realized how true they were. "Now, will you get out of the car? I could really use a break."

Slowly Ally climbed out. "Where are we going?"

"Let's try a little sightseeing."

Grudgingly, Ally walked alongside Kate. They caught up with Riley and headed toward the Acropolis. Everything looked the same, as far as Kate could tell, other than the huge metal frame in the shape of a Christmas tree at the top of the hill that some workers were stringing with lights.

"It's hard to believe it's almost Christmas," Ally said, sounding sad. No doubt her thoughts were tracking back to Jenny.

"You'll be home before the holiday." Kate squeezed her shoulders. "I'm sure of it."

Slowly but surely Ally loosened up. The moment she saw the stately, awe-inspiring Parthenon, her bored expression turned to one of pure delight. Smiling from ear to ear, she moved from one site to another, reading, asking questions and snapping off photos with the disposable camera Riley had bought for her in the first gift shop they happened upon.

Kate had loved exploring this city on her own when she'd come to Athens with Maggie all those years ago. Revisiting the ruins with Riley and Ally now, and watching them interact, turned out to be even more enjoyable. Riley was a much better father than he gave himself credit for. After several hours traipsing around the ruins with the midday sun warming the cool breeze coming off the Mediterranean, they were all sunburned and in need of a break.

"Let's head to the Plaka market," Kate said. "It's pretty there and shaded and there are lots of tourist shops."

"Yes!" Ally exclaimed. "Shopping."

"This is the oldest part of the city," Kate explained once they reached the Plaka district.

"Looks like it," Riley said, glancing around.

Within moments the smells of roasted chicken and lemon mixed with the scent of olive trees assailed her senses. Memories of being in Greece with Maggie flooded her mind. That had been such a turbulent time in Kate's life. She'd been struggling to stand on her own two feet, to make her own decisions all while Maggie had been stuck in control mode. So when she'd met Riley, her fists had already been clenched for a fight. In some ways she wished she and Riley could start over again. Start fresh without any preconceived notions about each other.

But that wasn't going to happen.

"Suddenly I'm starving," Riley said. "Let's get something to eat."

They walked down the sidewalk and ordered spicy souvlaki, lamb kabobs, corn on the cob, pistachios and freshly squeezed lemonade from street vendors. As they ate, they strolled the narrow alleyways, many shaded from the unrelenting sun by tall, lush trees and other greenery.

One small shop followed another and another, selling everything from old musical instruments to bronze and ceramic reproductions of ancient statues, monuments and ruins. Scarves and dresses, hats and jewelry, wind chimes, oils and candles. Handcrafted arts. Kiosks selling newspapers, magazines, gum and candy. A street musician stood in the shade squeezing an accordion and singing a folk song. Sidewalk cafés with window boxes filled with still-colorful flowers. Vines clung to the sides of the old buildings.

As the afternoon passed, Ally looked more and more relaxed. She was smiling, laughing and chatting away, forgetting for a few hours that her aunt's life was in jeopardy.

Riley, on the other hand, had barely let down his guard. He was forever checking the position of the setting sun or glancing at his watch, waiting. It wasn't long after they'd finished eating that Ally found a shop full of trendy teenager stuff.

She popped inside and he turned to Kate. "What did you say to Ally back at the parking lot by the Acropolis?"

"That you'd never let anything happen to Jenny. That she'll be safe."

"That's it?"

Kate hesitated. "I told her about my mom dying when I was eight. My dad leaving before I was born."

"You two have some common ground to stand on."

"It would appear so."

"I find myself again in the position of needing to thank you."

"You don't need to thank me for anything."

"I do." He looked at her, held her gaze. "Ally needed these few hours to decompress, and I wouldn't have been able to make that happen on my own."

"Riley, I think you'd be truly surprised at what you're capable of when it comes to Ally." But what she was really starting to wonder about was what he was capable of when it came to *her*.

It was that kiss. Pretending it hadn't happened wasn't working. She wanted to kiss him again. And more.

"Kate," Ally said, excited. "Come and look."

Good thing Ally was there.

"Coming," Kate said, finding the girl inside the

shop. Before they moved on, Kate bought Ally sunglasses, a necklace with small gold Greek-coin pendants strung along the chain, and a pair of handcrafted leather sandals.

The next shop they ventured into stocked clothes and accessories for all ages, but dusk had begun to settle. While Riley stood watching them, Kate and Ally dived into the shop, talking and laughing.

"Oh, you'd look so cute in this," Ally said, holding out a bright pink patterned dress.

"You think?" Kate said, eyeing it. "I don't usually wear pink."

"Try it on."

Kate snatched it off the rack, went into a change room, then stepped out to model the garment.

"C-u-u-ute," Ally said.

"I'm not sure." Kate glanced at herself in the mirror.

"Dad, tell her." Ally grabbed his arm. "Doesn't she look gorgeous in that dress?"

Clearly uncomfortable, Riley studied Kate. Up and down and down and up. "You're asking me? What do I know about fashion?"

"You know what looks nice on women. Does the dress look good on Kate? All you have to say is yes or no."

"Yes."

"See?" Ally said smugly.

But it was the intense way Riley was looking

at Kate that captured her attention. As if he was tracking her thoughts, his gaze flicked to her lips, and he seemed to grow more tense.

Ally disappeared down an aisle and they were quite suddenly left alone. Standing close to each other. Too close.

"It's time we got back to Angelo's house," Riley muttered.

"I know."

"Kate—"

"Do you love her?" The thought came out of nowhere. The question out of her mouth before she could swallow it back.

"Who?"

"Jenny."

"Jenny?" He tilted his head at her, narrowed his eyes. "I love her. Like family. But I'm not *in* love with my sister-in-law. Not even close."

"It's just that she's probably so much like your wife. I thought…"

"Kate—"

"I know. I know." She held up her hand, embarrassed. "You're not a family man. But when I see you with Ally…I wonder."

"Don't. You can wonder all you want. It's not going to change anything."

CHAPTER ELEVEN

"OKAY, THIS IS IT." Riley put down his binoculars and glanced at his watch. "Angelo should be leaving the house any minute, and the guard just finished patrolling this side of the property. I've got about fifteen minutes before his next pass."

"Dad, I want to help." Ally sat forward from the back and rested her arms along the front seat.

"No, Ally," he said. "You and Kate need to stay in the car." The sun had set some time ago and they'd been parked only a block from Angelo's fully walled and gated property, watching and waiting.

"Wait a minute." Kate turned toward him. "You can't do this one alone."

"I know I can help," Ally added. "I've heard you and Kate talking about it. There's got to be something I can do."

Two women. Double the chaos. What Riley wouldn't have given for a couple of the guys, someone who knew how to take orders. He dug deep inside for some patience. "I won't lie to either of you. This is dangerous. But this isn't a lie, either.

Having you along would make it more dangerous for me. So stay put. I'll be back in no time."

"Riley, when are you going to get it through that thick head of yours that I can help you? You need me. If for no other reason than to ID the statue."

She was right, but it didn't sit well.

"I'll be quiet," she said. "I'll follow you. I'll do exactly as you say."

That'd be the day. He glanced from Kate to Ally. Maybe it was time they both learned how to take orders, and he needed something to keep Ally in the car. That was the only way to keep her safe.

"All right. Kate, you're coming with me. Put this on." He tossed her his black jacket. He'd changed into a long-sleeved black T-shirt, but she needed something to cover her pale, reflective skin. "Ally, you watch the house and the driveway. If you see any movement, anything at all, you call me." He handed Ally one of the phones and a set of binoculars.

"Kate and I are going to hop over the wall and wait in the bushes until Angelo leaves." He gave Ally the phone number and further directions. "As soon as Angelo's gone, we'll be ready to make our move. The instant you see vehicle headlights start toward the road, call me on my cell. I'll have it on vibrate." He didn't really need her call, but if it made Ally happy to help, so be it. "Got it?"

"Got it."

"As soon as we leave this car, you lock the doors. Then you watch the house. I'll leave the keys here, but you are not to leave this vehicle unless there is an emergency and you have no other options." As long as she stayed put, she'd be safe. "Understand?"

"Yes." She nodded. "How long before you're back?"

"It'll take us no more than an hour, but if we're gone five hours you *still* don't leave this car. I'll call you if there's a problem. But if I don't, you fall asleep and wait until morning. Can you do that?"

"Yes." Such a little thing, but Ally looked proud to be of some use. Maybe this wasn't such a bad idea.

"Good." Soon after they'd landed in Athens, Riley had secured several weapons from another of March's contacts, as well as equipment he'd need to disable Angelo's security system. This time, unlike in Italy, he'd located March's tracking device and destroyed it. He dug through the bag, grabbed what he needed, then glanced back at Ally. "One more thing."

"What?"

"You need to remember that stealing is wrong."

Ally rolled her eyes and glanced at Kate. Kate was clearly trying to hold back a smile. There was no doubt these two joining forces would make a lesser man turn tail and run for the hills. "The only reason I'm doing this is for Jenny's sake."

"I'm not an idiot, Dad."

"I know that. I needed to do my dad thing, okay?"

"Would you go already?"

As Kate climbed out onto the sidewalk, Riley glanced one more time at Ally. There was so much he wanted to say to her, so much he wanted to share, but now was not the time.

He hoped they still *had* time.

With no further discussion, Riley got out of the car, made sure Ally locked the door, then walked with Kate along the wall enclosing Angelo's property. The sky was partly cloudy, providing only intermittent moonlight, so Riley moved slowly and made sure they weren't being watched. A warm breeze blew past them, bringing with it the scent of lemon trees and olive groves.

"Here." He stopped at the far corner. "This is where we hop over the wall."

"Hop?" She gawked at him. "This cement wall is six feet tall."

"I'll lift you." He put out his hands, fingers interlocking. "When you get to the other side, crouch down against the wall and stay put." They'd know within a few minutes whether or not the camera blind spot had been fixed.

She was heavier than she looked, but with good upper-body strength. One boost from him and she hoisted herself over the wall within seconds. Riley quickly followed and glanced toward the camera in the corner. The camera was new, but he could tell by looking at it that they were outside its range. No one had adjusted its arc. They were in the clear.

"Now we wait," he whispered, dropping into the shadows between several bushes and the rough outer wall.

"For how long?" she whispered back.

"As long as it takes."

"What do we do if Angelo doesn't leave?"

"He'll leave." Angelo had to leave. If he didn't, things got very complicated. Riley pointed next to him and held out a black ski mask. "Get down here and put this on."

"Yes, sir," Kate whispered, crouching next to him.

He pulled on his own mask. "Here comes that attitude again."

"Why is it that seemingly strong men are so threatened by women with attitude?"

Riley kept his mouth firmly closed on that one.

"Take you, for example." She drew the mask over her head. "You're a confident guy. Why is it you like quiet and accommodating women?"

Talk about treading on thin ice.

"Well?"

He glanced at her and immediately regretted it. The mask, rather than hiding her features, served only to heighten the ones he could see. Her eyes looked bigger and a richer amber color. Her lips more full and bowed. Better to keep his eyes off Kate and on the lookout instead for the guard. "Can't go wrong with quiet and accommodating." Was he trying to convince her or himself?

"Well, since I'm neither of those, I think it's safe to say that's why I never get past the third date."

He couldn't believe they were talking about this, but who knew how long they'd be waiting? For a soldier hunkered down and waiting, sometimes quiet conversation was all there was to pass the time.

"Kate, don't take this the wrong way, but you're a beautiful woman. You're smart. Sexy. High-spirited, strong and willful," he continued. "And it very well could be you haven't gotten past the third date with a man because you're hanging with the wrong type of guy. You're too much for the men you've been dating. You haven't found one who deserves you."

"Well, Riley," she said, a smile in her voice, "that sounded an awful lot like a compliment."

"Maybe it was." Suddenly uncomfortable, he shifted positions.

"All right. Since you're so smart, what kind of man should I be dating?"

"You can hold your own with any man. Don't be afraid of a man tough enough to meet you head-to-head."

"You mean like you?" she whispered.

"No," he said, shaking his head. "Nothing like me. I'm about as wrong for you as a man can get."

"Why?"

"Because I…" For the first time in this discussion, he faltered. He'd boxed himself in. "You want a man *like* me, Kate, but you don't want *me*." He put a finger of one hand to his mouth as he pointed with the other. "Shh. Don't move."

Riley never took his eyes off the guard as they silently waited for him to pass, then he glanced at his watch. Angelo was late. He should've left at least five minutes ago. A moment later the guard had moved out of earshot.

"Then again," he whispered, continuing where they'd left off, "it could be that you haven't gotten past the third date because you've got it in your head that you've got to break up with the guy before the guy breaks up with you."

A puff of air left her lips.

"Hit a nerve?"

"Hardly."

"Sulking?"

"I don't sulk," she said. "You said it yourself, Riley. I haven't gotten serious with a guy because I want to get married. Have kids. Settle down. What's the point in wasting time with a man who doesn't want the same things I want?"

"Which is exactly why you shouldn't waste any time on me."

"You know, all those years ago," she whispered. "When you escorted me from Greece back home to D.C.?"

Oh, hell.

"I might've had a crush on you, but I'll bet you didn't even know I existed, did you?"

"Oh, I knew you existed, all right." He chuckled, soft and low. "Let's say a certain swarm of butterflies is branded in my memory, and leave it at that."

"End of discussion?" Now it was her turn to chuckle.

He signaled to Kate to be quiet as the guard came near for another pass. That's when voices came from the front of the house. Car doors slammed and a moment later an engine roared to life and headlights shone down the short, winding drive. Thank God. Angelo was leaving.

The guard moved out of earshot as Riley's cell phone vibrated. He flicked it open and whispered, "Ally? Everything okay?"

"Fine," she whispered back. "I saw headlights. It looks like the car is coming."

"Thanks." He flipped it closed. "We're almost ready."

A moment later Angelo's Mercedes cruised through the gate and pulled onto the street. After the gate closed, Riley handed Kate a gun. "The safety's off, so don't pull the trigger unless you intend to do some damage. And if you have to shoot, don't aim directly at anyone. I might know the guard."

Kate took a deep breath.

"You sure you want to do this?"

She nodded.

"Okay. Sit tight for a minute. I'm going to mess with the security camera in that corner." He pointed toward the one closest to them. "There will be a guard monitoring the camera feed, but by knocking out this one, they'll have an even bigger blind spot. He'll come out to fix it and when he does, I'll take care of him."

"You sure this will work?"

"No, but Angelo overprotects his grounds. These guards get bored out of their minds when year after year they see no action. I'm hoping he won't know what hit him."

Sliding close against the wall, Riley carefully crept toward the corner security camera. He cut off a branch from a nearby tree, flicked it in front of the camera a few times before settling the leaves directly in front of the lens, obscuring the view. Then he snipped the main wire. They managed to make it to the garage before a side door opened and the security guard stepped outside. Carrying a flashlight and tool kit, the man took a quick look around and headed for the failed camera.

Riley came behind him, overpowered him and within minutes had the man back in the security room off the garage, handcuffed and gagged.

"Okay, let's move," Riley said, entering the house. "I want to get back to Ally as fast as we can."

They made it through the staff kitchen and out into the main area of the house, but when they reached the art displays in the dining room there was no statue to be found.

"I don't see it," Kate said, glancing again at every shelf.

"You're sure?"

"Positive."

"Let's check the rest of the house. It's got to be here somewhere."

They checked the formal living room and found no ancient art. Next they went down the hall and into the library. There were some very expensive pieces, no doubt, but no ancient Greek representation of the primordial god Chaos.

"It's not anywhere," Kate whispered.

"Stop!" a man called behind them. "Drop your weapons or I will shoot to kill!"

CHAPTER TWELVE

KATE DROPPED HER GUN and spun around. Riley slowly turned. A skinny old man, wearing a newsboy cap and glasses, held Ally tightly by the arm. He looked harmless enough, but that was more than she could say for the two security guards standing on either side of him with guns aimed directly at her and Riley.

"You, American," one of the guards said, his Greek accent thick and strong. "I said drop your weapon."

Riley hesitated as if he was assessing the guards' capabilities, then he finally set his gun on a nearby table.

"Now put up your hands," the guard said. "*Sigá.* Slowly."

"Daddy, I'm sorry," Ally cried. "He made me tell him about you. I know you told me not to get out of the car, but he made me—"

"It's all right, honey. You didn't do anything wrong."

"Take off those masks," the old man said.

Kate immediately tugged hers off. Riley slowly

followed suit and glanced at Kate. "I'm sorry I got you into this."

"You didn't."

The old man came forward a few steps. "*Yiatí?* Why? What are you…" He paused and squinted at Riley. "James Riley. What in Zeus's name are you doing here?"

"*Hérete,* Angelo," Riley said. "Hello."

"Why have you broken in to my house?"

"It's a long story."

"So are you going to kill me?" he asked softly.

"You know I wouldn't."

"Put down your guns," he told his men.

They hesitated.

"Drop them. Now," he said. "Everything is fine." He released Ally, and she ran to Riley.

"It's all right, honey." Not taking his eyes off Angelo, Riley hugged her and kept his arm around her as he faced his old friend. For a moment they all stood awkwardly in the room, glancing at each other. "How did you know we were here?" Riley asked.

"We passed by your car on the street," Angelo said. "I noticed a young girl sitting in the backseat alone and it was worrying me. Funny, but I had my driver turn around to make sure she was okay." He tossed the keys to one of his men. "*Parakaló.*

Please, Stamos, bring Riley's car up to the house now."

After the men had disappeared, Angelo tossed his cap onto the hall table, shrugged out of his jacket and held his hands out to his sides. "So. As they say, an open enemy is better than a false friend."

"I am not your enemy, Angelo."

"No? Then are you going to explain this to me?"

"David March," Riley said. "That enough explanation for the moment?"

"For the moment." Angelo looked toward Ally. "Who's this?"

"My daughter," Riley said. "Ally."

"I should've known." He patted Ally's cheek and smiled softly at her. "You must look like your mother."

Ally smiled.

"And this one?" Angelo asked, referring to Kate. "I feel as though I should know her."

Riley stepped back so Angelo could get a good look at her. "You probably don't remember—"

"Na, ah, ah." Angelo put up his hand and smiled at Kate. "I know. I know. Maggie Ballos's sister, Kate."

"You remember me?" Kate asked.

He shrugged. "Nick and Maggie send e-mails.

You're in many of the photos." He glanced at Riley. "How long will you be in Athens?"

"One night."

Angelo looked back and forth between the three of them. Suddenly he said, "Then you must stay here with us."

Riley shook his head. "We have to leave—"

"James. I will not argue. I've told you time and time again, although I know that you never believed me, my home is your home. Nadi is asleep now, but she'd shoot me for sure if she wakes up in the morning and finds out I had you three in our home and didn't make you stay."

"All right. For Nadi."

"You can take your daughter to the first guest bedroom on the left." While Riley was gone, Angelo directed Kate toward the couches in the recessed living area and went to the bar. They chatted about Nick and Maggie and the kids as he opened a bottle of red wine, brought three glasses to the table and filled them one by one.

Riley came back a moment later and Angelo glanced at him. "So tell me. Why did you break in to my home?"

"Angelo, you don't want to get involved in this."

"It's a little late for that, isn't it?"

Riley rubbed his eyes. "David March kidnapped my sister-in-law and will kill her if I don't cooperate with him."

"March." Angelo barely reacted. "One of these days someone is going to give that man what's coming to him."

"With any luck, that man will be me, but first I need to get my sister-in-law to safety."

"What does Kate have to do with this?"

"I have an expertise in identifying and repairing certain ancient artifacts," Kate said. "I'm here to help Riley."

"March wants you to steal something from me, *né?*"

"Yes."

"Are you going to tell me what, or do you still plan to steal it out from under me?"

Riley sat on the couch next to Kate. "You own a statue. It's one of five he wants me to steal."

"The primordial deity Chaos," Kate explained. "From the Hellenistic period."

Angelo frowned at them. "Then we have a problem."

"Don't do this, Angelo," Riley said. "Let me borrow it. I swear. I'll get it back to you. Somehow. Some way."

"I know you would, James. I know." Angelo scratched his head, dislodging several wisps of long, silky gray hair, and took a slow sip of wine. "Unfortunately I can't give you the statue."

"That complicates things." Riley clenched his jaw and glanced around the room as if his gaze could not rest for a moment.

"Don't do that," Angelo said. "Don't start plotting ways to take me down. It won't do you any good."

"You're not giving me much of a choice."

"James, you're an honest man. I know you don't think much of it, but you helped me out of more than one jam." Angelo took a deep breath. "If I had the statue, I would give it to you. But I no longer own it."

Riley stared at him. "Who does?"

"No one." He took a sip of wine. "Last summer, my sister had an important dinner party at her house in the northern suburbs. She wanted to display some of my art, hoping to impress those in attendance. A few days later, before I could collect my pieces, the fires ravaging Athens at the time quickly reached her neighborhood. In a matter of hours her home was burned to the ground. She saved only the items she thought were the most valuable, not realizing the statue of Chaos should've been one of them. The fire burned so hot, the figure was completely destroyed."

"Oh, my God," Kate murmured, glancing at Riley.

"This won't change anything as far as March

is concerned." Riley held Kate's gaze. "He'll kill Jenny if he doesn't get that statue."

"You said Trace will find a way to get Jenny safe," Kate said. "We just need to stall March."

"That's not good enough. I have to be working this from both ends. To be safe." Riley stood and paced the room. "Angelo, does anyone have the details of what you lost in the fire?"

"*Óhi,*" Angelo explained. "No one knows. I came by the statue and several other pieces in a… let's say…questionable fashion."

"Then we've got a chance." Riley glanced at Kate. "We're going to pretend we have it."

"*Pós?*" Angelo asked. "How?"

"By bluffing. It's our only option."

"No, there's something else we can do," Kate said, holding Riley's gaze. "I can make a replica. It won't be perfect, but it should fool all but the most trained eyes."

"How long will that take?" Riley asked.

"It's a slow process. Molding, drying, carving. Firing it in a kiln. Under normal circumstances several weeks."

"Kate, we don't have that much time."

"I know." She ran her hands through her tangled hair, thinking. "Theoretically, the clay would need at least two days to dry before being fired in a kiln. It'll probably take me two days to make it. I need four days."

"You've got two. I have to leave for Moscow no later than Friday. Waiting even that long will give me only one day to steal the last two statues."

"What can I do to help?" Angelo offered.

"Give me a space to work," Kate said, standing. "I need a countertop and good lighting."

"What else do you need?" Riley came toward her.

"To get at it right away."

RILEY WATCHED KATE line things up on the work-table in the well-lit room Angelo had showed them to after Kate had gathered her supplies. She laid out several pictures Angelo had given her of the actual figurine he'd owned as well as images she'd printed off the Internet. She also set out the other two statues they'd stolen in Ostia and dropped the bag of clay she'd brought with her from D.C. onto the counter along with some tools.

"Is there anything else you need from me?" Angelo asked.

"No," Kate said. "Thank you, Angelo."

"Then I will let you both get to it."

"Angelo," Riley said, causing the older man to look back. "Thank you, and I apologize for taking you away from Diloti tonight."

"Ah. No bother. It's a card game." He grinned. "I'll beat them all next week."

After Angelo had left, Riley paced beside the counter. "What can I do to help?"

"Nothing. This is going to take some time."

He folded his arms over his chest. "I don't know how to do nothing."

She glanced at him, concern filling her gaze. "Then learn." She scooped the hunk of clay out of the bag and slapped it onto the counter.

"Would it be possible for you to make replicas of the statues in Russia?"

"I don't have enough time or enough clay."

He glanced down at the lump she was working over and over with the heels of her hands. "That's not enough for one statue."

"I know, Riley. That's why I asked one of Angelo's men to get some more before we came down here."

"What if it's not the right color or texture?"

"I can guarantee it won't be. This clay we brought from the museum in D.C., remember? It was mixed especially for these statues."

He ran his hands through his short hair. "So what—"

"Riley, stop." Kate came around the table and put her hands on his chest. "I'll layer the special clay over the clay the guard brings back. I'm very good at making replicas. That's why museums hire me. I will do everything within my power to make sure this statue is right."

"I know you will, Kate," he whispered. Before giving himself a moment to think better of it, he ran his hand along the side of her face.

Slowly she closed her eye and leaned into his touch.

If only this nightmare was over. If only Jenny was safe and he and Kate had nothing hanging over their heads. He'd take her into his arms and he'd— No, he wouldn't. There was still the matter of them having no future between them. He was not who she needed in a man.

But what did *he* want? To go back to active duty once this was all said and done and carry on as before? For Ally to go back to living with Jenny? For him to live and die a soldier with no more depth to him and his life than one of these Greek statues?

As he ran the pad of his thumb over Kate's lips, he wasn't so sure of the answers to any of those questions. The only thing he knew for sure was that he wanted to feel this woman's lips against his mouth one more time.

Wrapping his hand behind Kate's neck, he bent and kissed her. He urged her lips open and gently explored her mouth with his tongue. On an achy sigh, she wrapped her arms around him and he lifted her against him.

She felt solid and strong for such a small package, and that more than anything turned him on.

Surprisingly, the last thing he found himself wanting from Kate was anything sweet or soft. Slanting his mouth, he deepened their kiss.

She groaned, ran her hands under his shirt, proving to him how much he wanted her, and at that moment he realized that come hell or high water, he was going to have her. But not like this. Not with this missing Chaos statue hanging over their heads.

He pulled back, set her down and stepped away. "Kate…"

"I swear to God, Riley, you are just like every other man I've ever known. Too weak for a strong woman." She looked away. "Get out of here, okay?"

"Kate—"

"Let me do this."

She was wrong about him being weak, but until this was over, he needed to keep his distance. "Okay," he whispered. "You'll—"

"Let you know if I need anything. I swear." She took him by the arm, led him across the room and pushed him out into the hall. "Go!"

He stood there a moment after she shut the door in his face. Restless and preoccupied, he went back upstairs and out into the living room. Angelo had gone to bed after showing him to a guest bedroom. He turned toward the room and noticed Ally's light on, although the door was closed. She was still awake.

So what? She'll be fine. She'll deal. Besides, he'd tried reconnecting at the airport, and Ally was having none of it. He had turned and taken several steps when the sound of sniffling stopped him. She wasn't fine.

Don't avoid her. Be the father she needs.

He rapped softly on the door.

"What?"

Cracking open the door, he found her sitting out on the balcony, a late-night breeze blowing through her long hair as she stared out over the city. "Ally? You okay?"

"I'm fine," she whispered, turning her head to wipe the corner of her eye.

"You don't look fine." He sat on the chair next to her.

"You've got bigger problems than me."

"Hey," he said, pausing, trying to frame his words in the best way he knew how. "I know this is going to be hard for you to believe, but you're the most important thing in my world. No matter how small your problems are, they're big to me."

For a moment she seemed to be judging his sincerity. "I wanna go home, Dad. I'm sick of driving for hours, flying into foreign countries and sleeping in strange beds. And I'm sick of being scared." A tear slipped down her cheek, then another, and soon it was a steady stream. "But more than any-thing, I'm worried about Jenny. I miss her."

He couldn't fix this. A sense of frustration boiled up inside him. It killed him, but there wasn't any-thing he could do to fix this. Capable of nothing more substantial, he reached out to hug her and before he knew it, she was in his lap and he was rocking her like a big, overgrown baby.

A long time passed before she finally ran out of steam. She rubbed her swollen eyes with her hands. "I got your shirt all wet."

"I'll dry." He gave her shoulders a tight squeeze. "Ally, you need to believe this. I will not let any-thing happen to you."

She swallowed. "I know, Dad. What about Jenny?"

"Trace is going to do everything he can to get her back. As soon as an opportunity presents itself, he'll be all over March and his men. In a couple of days this is all going to feel like a bad nightmare. It's all going to work out. You'll see."

He could see her relax, her eyelids turn heavy. He carried her to the bed. In a few minutes she was sound asleep.

Was it possible this lame attempt at comfort was all she'd needed from him? Was it possible he could be the father she needed? And the biggest question of all—was it too late?

CHAPTER THIRTEEN

Thursday, 7:45 a.m.

VASILI BELOV...ties to a Moscow brotherhood of crime...investigated by the United States government...linked to the murder of a high court judge... under suspicion of smuggling nuclear weapons... cocaine...illegal oil trade...

Unlike the cold snap in D.C., unseasonably warm temperatures for late November were hitting Athens, so Riley sat at the table on the Bebels' patio and scanned through anything and everything he could find on the internet regarding the owner of the last two statues. If this information was any indication, Riley was in deep shit.

He pulled out his cell phone and connected to a saved number. A voice-mail system answered. "Roman, it's Riley," he said, leaving a message. "Call me ASAP. I need your help."

More worried than ever about Jenny, he closed the laptop Angelo had lent him and walked to the patio railing to look out over the city of Athens. A steady breeze blew away most of the normal overlying smog, so the view of the city center, including the Acropolis, was fairly clear. The ocean, dark blue and vast, stretched onward in the distance.

It was beautiful, picturesque, and all he wanted was to get out of Athens. The sooner he got to Moscow, the sooner he could get to Turkey and the sooner he could be done with March, get Jenny back and put this entire mess behind him. And then what?

His relationship with Ally was changing. Did he have the balls to take a step forward with his daughter, or was he going to do what he always did and take two steps back by pretending everything was the same as before?

Fine. Everything was just fine.

But it wasn't.

For so many years he'd been content, if not completely fulfilled with his career in the military, but for years restlessness had been building inside him to the point that he no longer knew what he wanted for his future.

And Kate? He didn't even want to think about her, the messiest piece of this whole deal. At least she'd been easy to avoid, cloistered as she'd been all morning in the lower-level workroom. He hadn't seen her since just after dawn. She'd woken within a few minutes of him and come into the kitchen right after he'd made a pot of coffee. After he'd handed her a cup, she'd silently disappeared downstairs.

He could get out now and head to Russia, leaving Kate here to finish the Chaos statue. But what if there was something else she needed? What if some problem developed in replicating that clay figure? He had to wait it out. No way around it.

The patio door opened behind him and Riley turned to find Nadi coming toward him, her arms outstretched. "*Kali méra,* James. It's so good to see you. You look so well. The years have been good to you."

He wasn't so sure about that. "*Hérete,* Nadi." He returned her hug and stepped back, uncomfortable as usual with her lavish shows of affection.

Her long, thick black hair, now streaked with gray, was pulled back into a clip at her nape. Her face had lost most of the plumpness that had once given her a youthful appearance. "Are you well?" he asked.

"Oh, *étsi k'étsi.* So-so. I've had my ups and downs these past years, like everyone else. A bout with cancer some time ago took a lot out of me."

"But you're doing all right now?"

"Cured. So they say. Since then, though, Angelo and I never take a single day for granted. We cherish our friends, present and past, more than ever. It's good to see you."

No wonder Angelo had been so open and friendly.

At that moment Angelo came out onto the patio carrying a tray filled with traditional Greek breakfast items. In the bright morning light the man's wrinkles seemed more pronounced.

"Let me help you with that, Angelo." Riley took the tray and nudged the patio door closed.

"Let's sit and visit." As if his joints ached, Angelo slowly lowered himself onto a chair.

Riley set the tray on the table and they enjoyed thick, heavy Greek coffee, honey with bread, chilled melon and fresh homemade spanakopita, a phyllo pastry filled with egg, spinach, feta cheese, onions and spices. The best part about his stay in Greece all those years ago had been Nadi's cooking.

"Angelo tells me your daughter is here," Nadi said. "I would like to meet her. Where is she?"

"Still sleeping. Angelo put us up in your guest bedrooms. I hope that's all right."

"I wouldn't have had it any other way. And Kate? Maggie's sister?"

"Downstairs. In Angelo's workroom."

"Well, I will have to meet her as soon as she can take a break."

While they ate and soaked up some of the bright morning sunshine, they caught up on each other's lives. He enjoyed hearing about their children and grandchildren, some of whom he'd met years ago. Filling them in on the events of Ally's life was cathartic for Riley. Maybe he hadn't been as absent as he'd thought.

"Ally must bring you great joy," Nadi said.

"She's a terrific kid."

They'd been visiting for some time when the cell phone March had given Riley rang. "*Signómi*, Nadi and Angelo. Excuse me. I must take this." Not wanting to take the chance of Ally overhearing by going inside the house and lacking a more private option, he stood, went to the rail and turned his back on his hosts. He flicked the phone open. "What?"

"Miss me?" March asked, his voice quiet and entirely too confident.

"Screw you."

"Ah, ah, ah. Get nasty with me and I won't let you talk to Jenny."

"Put her on the phone."

"After you give me an update." March paused. "Have you acquired both statues from Ostia?"

"Yes."

"Where are you now?"

"Let me talk to Jenny."

"You're not being very cooperative. I may have to take that into consideration next time Jenny needs to be…fed."

"You mistreat her, March, and I swear to God—"

"You'll what?" March yelled over the line. "If you'd called me when you'd reached Athens, and if you hadn't removed the tracking devices after picking up supplies yesterday, we wouldn't need to be having this conversation now, would we?"

Riley bit back the barrage of foul comments running through his mind. "All you need is the statues," he said, keeping the tone of his voice firmly under control. "You have no reason to track my every move."

"Because I want to is reason enough," March said. "Do you have Bebel's statue yet?"

"No. I've been monitoring his house. I'll have it by tomorrow."

"Now, that wasn't so hard, was it?"

Riley couldn't keep his hands from clenching into fists. There was a moment of silence, and then a soft feminine voice said, "James?"

"Jenny. Are you okay?"

"I'm fine. Ally?"

"She's good. Don't worry about us. Is March treating you well?"

"They're leaving me alone. I get food, water, sleep. I'll be fine—"

"That's enough," March said, back on the line. "Put Kate on."

"She's taking a shower."

An uneasy moment of silence hung between them.

"Would you like me to have her call you back?" Riley asked in as sarcastic a tone as he could conjure.

"Not necessary," March said. "My contact verified that she was with you yesterday. Call me when you get to Moscow."

The line went dead.

It was all Riley could do not to throw March's phone straight down Lykavitós hill. Sucking in a deep breath, he stuffed it into his pocket and turned back around to find Nadi and Angelo watching him. The concerned expressions on their faces said loud and clear that they'd likely heard most of his side of the conversation.

"Be careful," Angelo said quietly. "Danger gleams like sunshine in a brave man's eyes."

"I'm not looking for trouble, Angelo. Jenny's safety is all I'm after." Briefly he explained what was going on.

"Is there anything we can do?" Nadi asked.

"Thank you, Nadi, *efharistó*. But you and Angelo have already done more than enough."

"You could take a couple of my men with you to Moscow," Angelo suggested. "Or they could meet you in Turkey."

"I appreciate the offer, but I'm not sure that would do any good."

"Do you need weapons, supplies?"

"I have a contact in Moscow, but do you know someone in Istanbul?"

"I can set something up. You will have everything you need."

"Thank you." He glanced from one face to another. "And there is one more thing, if you don't mind."

"Name it."

"Can Ally and Kate stay here with you until this is over?"

They glanced at each other.

"*Málista*. Absolutely," Nadi said. "I'm sure your daughter will be no trouble, and I look forward to getting to know Maggie's sister."

"If anything should happen to me and Jenny, my parents—"

"We'll make sure Ally makes it safely to your family," Angelo said.

"But you must come back from Istanbul," Nadi whispered. "That's simply all there is to it."

"Well, I've had about all I can take of sitting around and waiting," Riley said. "Angelo, let's go fix your surveillance system. You've got a blind spot I want to show you."

KATE PUT DOWN HER TOOLS and rubbed her eyes. She felt nearly cross-eyed from focusing on this statue. She'd roughed up the basic shape within a couple of hours last night. Unable to keep her eyes open after that, she'd caught several hours of sleep and was awake this morning before everyone except Riley.

Riley. Her feelings for him were getting so confusing that the moment after he'd poured her a cup of coffee she'd gone straight to the lower level to get back at creating Chaos. It was ironic that chaos was exactly what she felt every time she thought of him. She couldn't believe he remembered her butterfly tattoos. That had been perhaps the most disturbing part of last night, learning that she actually had made an impression on him all those years ago when he'd escorted her home from Greece.

And still he'd left. Just like her father. Like Rufus. He was going to leave her again. When this business with March was all said and done, the same way Riley had abandoned his daughter, he was going to abandon her. There was no way around it.

Kate glanced at the clock. It was early for lunch, but she was starving and needed a boost. On leaving the workroom, she found Ally in the kitchen with an older woman Kate had never met. They were eating lunch in the breakfast nook. "Hey, Ally." Kate rubbed the girl's shoulder. "How are you doing?"

"I'm great." Smiling, she appeared more relaxed

than she'd been since all this had started. "Have you met Nadi?"

"You must be Kate Dillon," the woman said, standing. "I'm Nadi Bebel, Angelo's wife."

"Nice to meet you." Kate shook her hand. "I didn't mean to interrupt your lunch."

"No problem at all. Are you hungry?"

"Actually, I'm famished."

"Sit," Nadi said. "I'll get you something."

Kate sat across from Ally. While Nadi prepped Kate's lunch, she filled the older woman in on how Maggie, Nick and their three kids were doing.

"I've known Nick since he was a little boy," Nadi said, setting several plates in front of Kate with the makings for gyros—slices of spiced lamb, lettuce, tomatoes, onions, tzatziki sauce and pita bread. "I am so happy he found your Maggie." She brought over a large plate with a side salad of tomatoes, feta cheese, olives and onion tossed with dressing and then poured out three glasses of freshly squeezed lemonade.

"Me, too," Kate said. "They're perfect together."

The moment Nadi sat at the table to finish eating, Kate dived in. "So what have you been up to all morning?" she asked Ally.

"Watched some TV. Then Nadi took me shopping in the Kolonáki area."

The central Athens neighborhood, not far from Angelo's house, was set on the slopes of Mount

Lykavitós and was filled with trendy shops and restaurants. Kate regretted not being able to join them. She'd come to enjoy spending time with Ally. Having to say goodbye to Riley wouldn't be the only downside to putting an end to this deal with March.

"Then we went to a grocery store, and I helped her make lunch. She's been teaching me Greek."

"No kidding. What can you say?"

Ally pronounced several individual words as well as a few common phrases.

"Good job. Maybe later you can teach me." Kate smiled. "Do you know where your dad is?"

"He's outside with Angelo and one of the guards, fixing a security camera."

The one they'd broken last night.

"Angelo and I had breakfast with James early this morning outside on the patio," Nadi added. "He seems more grounded than he was all those years ago when you were here in Greece with Maggie. Maybe even happy."

"My dad?" Ally glanced at Nadi. "Happy?"

"*Né.* He is very different now from how I remember him. I worried about him back then. He was… quiet, almost to the point of being withdrawn."

She had that right. Kate took a bite of gyro to keep from mouthing off in front of Ally.

"Ally, your father is a very brave man."

"Yeah, I know."

"Do you?" Nadi smiled. "Well, I'll tell you, he's saved Angelo's life. Twice that I know of."

"Really? How?"

"The first time was in Kosovo. Angelo had inadvertently gotten involved in some business with a disreputable man. When Angelo refused the deal and left the building through the back door, Riley was there. He helped Angelo and his men out of that nasty situation."

"That's not how Riley described it," Kate said smiling wryly. "He says Angelo saved his life."

"*Né?*" Nadi raised her eyebrows. "He is being modest. Angelo has said countless times that if not for Riley, Angelo would be as dead as dirt. This from a man not prone to exaggeration. And still Riley came back with us to Greece, saying he owed Angelo his own life."

"That's when I first met him," Kate said.

Nadi stirred her lemonade. "He seemed so sad back then. All I wanted was to mother him. But then that was not long after your mother had died." Nadi glanced at Ally.

Ally picked at her lunch. "I wonder what would've happened if my mom had lived?"

Interesting question.

"I'll bet he would've stayed home more," Ally whispered. "So maybe if there was another woman. Maybe if he was dating someone…" She glanced at Kate with a suspicious glint in her eyes.

"Oh, no," Kate said, shaking her head. "Don't look at me."

Nadi chuckled.

"But you like him. I know you do." Ally studied Kate. "It would be okay with me if you and my dad…you know…checked each other out."

"Oh, it would, would it?" Kate couldn't help but smile.

"Yeah. I mean, I know he's not… I mean, I wouldn't call him hot. You'd never see him on the cover of some magazine or anything. He's only okay looking."

That showed how much thirteen-year-olds knew about grown men. As far as Kate was concerned, all the actors and male models of this world could keep their camera-ready good looks. They couldn't hold a candle to Riley's virility, his real-life handsomeness. "Let me tell you something, Ally. Your dad's a lot more than *okay looking*."

"You think? Like how?"

"I don't know." Kate looked away, feeling more than a little self-conscious. "He just is."

"He's kind of bossy, though, but you are, too, so you guys are perfect for each other."

"I'm not so sure about that." Kate laughed. "Most of the time we're more like oil and water."

"That's because he hasn't had a lot of practice with women. I don't think he's dated anyone since…well, since my mom died."

"He's never introduced you to any girl-friends?"

"Never. But he likes you." Ally grinned. "A lot."

Kate felt as if she was back in high school all over again, but she couldn't help herself. "You think?"

"Oh, yeah. He's never brought a date home, but I've seen the way he acts around women. I mean, I've never seen him actually listen to a woman before. Not the way he listens to you. You're smart, and I think he respects that. And you should see how he looks at, well…" Ally said, pausing. She started to chuckle and then laugh outright.

"What? How he looks at what?"

"You. When he thinks you're not looking. When you walk away. His eyes go all over you."

"Oh, stop." Kate glanced at Nadi, but the older woman's sly smile only seemed to encourage Ally all the more.

"I'm serious. He thinks you're hot." Ally's smile was more than a little conspiratorial. "So do you like him?"

The hopeful look on Ally's face was almost too much for Kate. "Honestly, Ally, I'm not sure what I feel for your dad." Kate chewed on a hangnail. "He…well, he confuses me."

"There's a boy at school that confuses me, too. Joel Tate."

"Do you like Joel?"

"One minute I'm arguing with him and the next I'm blushing because he looked at me."

Sounded an awful lot like what was happening between Kate and Riley.

"Well, I want you to know that if you do start to like my dad, I'm okay with that."

"It's good to know, Ally. And thank you." She glanced at Nadi. "Thank you for lunch. Now I have to get back to work."

And safer ground.

CHAPTER FOURTEEN

RILEY FIXED THE DAMAGE he'd caused to Angelo's security camera the previous night and also remounted a couple of the cameras in order to eliminate blind spots. As they took a final walk around the perimeter of the property, Riley said, "I think that should do it. Your estate is now about as secure as reasonably possible."

"Are you sure I can't talk you into working for me?" Angelo asked as they headed back to the house. "I think I'm almost ready to retire. I need someone to take over my business."

"Thanks for the offer, Angelo, but I won't live this far from Ally. Besides, I'm not sure I'm interested in an imports business."

His thoughts touched again on those retirement papers sitting on his desk back in D.C. He had enough put away in savings that with his military pension and benefits, he'd never have to work again, but he wasn't the type to laze around. The only way he could even consider retirement was if there was something to keep him busy. The idea of consulting on private security might interest him.

He imagined a civilian lifestyle, and Kate kept popping into the picture.

He hadn't seen her since first thing that morning and he was itching to see how she was doing on the clay figure. Oddly enough, he had to admit, there was a part of him that simply wanted to see *her*. All the more reason to stay busy.

"Is there anything else I can do for you?" Riley asked.

"No, we do okay here with most things the way they are. I hire too many guards to keep them all busy, I suppose, but their families need to eat, yes?"

Either Riley had been too young to appreciate Angelo's generous spirit or the man had mellowed over the years, possibly a bit of both.

"I'm guessing Nadi prepared an early lunch for us," Angelo said as they approached the house. "Are you hungry?"

"You know me. I can always eat."

They entered the kitchen to find Nadi at the counter. "Well, it's about time you two get back here," the older woman said.

"I hope you ate without us," Angelo said.

"Yes. Everything is still on the table for you and James."

Riley and Angelo sat and made themselves plump gyros from the makings Nadi had laid out for them. Riley had barely swallowed his last bite when Ally wandered into the kitchen, looking bored and restless.

"So, James? Ally?" Nadi said, glancing back and forth between the two of them. "What are you two going to do this afternoon?"

Riley looked toward his daughter.

Ally, though, glanced at Nadi. "Do you want to go shopping again?"

"Oh, dear, I'd truly love to do that with you, but I can't. I have a friend in the hospital I must visit this afternoon. Maybe your father can take you."

Ally looked toward him hopefully. "Dad, I know you don't like shopping much, so can we go do some more sightseeing?"

Even under the best of circumstances Riley was never much for company. Chances were he'd be downright uncommunicative, given the fact that he hated having to wait things out.

"You and I never do things alone," she said, pumping up the pressure. "If you really want to reconnect," she whispered so no one else could hear, "then show me."

How could he turn his back on that challenge? "Okay, Ally, let's go." It was probably best for him to steer clear of Kate anyway. "You got your walking shoes on?"

After getting the rundown of must-sees from Nadi and Angelo, they were out the door. Their first stop was the National Archaeological Museum.

They could've stayed there all day perusing arti-facts, statues and paintings and even come back the next day for more, but Ally wanted to see as much as she could. After a quick visit to the Temple of Zeus, they drove through Syntagma Square and around the National Garden.

They'd been alone together on a few vaca-tions when she'd been quite little, but this was the longest span of time Riley had hung with Ally the teenager. He was impressed by her avid interest in history, something he wouldn't have spent the time of day considering when he'd been her age, but she had a decisive, no-nonsense side that re-minded him so much of himself at her age it was a bit unnerving.

They enjoyed a dinner of fresh fish cooked in a lemon-and-caper sauce at a little sidewalk café in the Monastiraki street market not far from where he, Ally and Kate had shopped the other day. Then they were off to hit the Temple of Poseidon before sunset. They climbed to the top of the ruin and stood at the edge. The Aegean Sea was spread out below them like an endless swath of blue satin.

"It's pretty, isn't it, Dad?" she said.

"Gorgeous."

"Can we come back some day?"

"I don't see why not."

Standing next to Ally talking about the view, he was forced to admit this day had been one of the best days of his life. The only thing missing had been Kate. Maybe there should be more days like this, more time with Ally. Although he felt too young to retire from the military, he'd known countless others who'd done just that. Not a one had ever regretted his decision. Maybe it was time for his life to take an about-face.

"Excuse me," a young woman standing next to Riley said. "Would you take our picture?" She was with a young man.

"Sure." While Ally stood by, Riley took the woman's digital camera, framed the couple and snapped off a couple photos. Both were wearing wedding rings and looked happy and relaxed. As he handed back the camera, he asked, "On your honeymoon?"

"Yes." They looked at each other and smiled simultaneously.

"Congratulations."

"Thanks." The couple wandered away.

Ally was watching him as he turned back toward her. "Did you know Kate likes you?"

Riley chuckled. "She doesn't *like* like me."

"Yes. She does."

"She told you this?"

"I know she does."

"And how do you know?"

"Trust me. I know."

"You're telling me this because…"

"Oh, come on, Dad. Don't be so obtuse."

"Obtuse?" Smiling, he shook his head. "Okay, I won't."

"Do you like her?"

"I respect her. She's a good person." And yes, he realized, he did like Kate. "But there's no room in my life for a woman, Ally. You know that."

"Things change, Dad. You've changed. Maybe there's more room than you think."

BY THE TIME Riley and Ally made their way back to the Bebel home, it was still early evening, but Ally was exhausted. She did, however, manage to fill Angelo and Nadi in on all the excitement of the afternoon, before asking, "Where's Kate?"

"She came upstairs for dinner and a break here and there," Angelo explained. "But the rest of the time she's been downstairs working."

"Can I go see her, Dad?"

"Sure. Let's see what she's up to."

After Riley and Ally wished the Bebels a good night, they went downstairs to see Kate. At the doorway, he held Ally back to make sure they wouldn't be interrupting anything critical. For a moment he watched Kate work on the clay statue. So intent on her process, she had no clue they'd come into the room, no clue he was as mesmerized by her as she was by her work.

Sitting on a tall metal stool at the counter, she

held a wooden tool in her hand and was scraping away at the clay. Her lips puckered as she gently blew at the filings, but then she picked up a brush and softly flicked at something at the front midsection of the figure.

So serious and focused. So beautiful.

"Sit like that much longer," he said, "and you may not be able to unbend."

She glanced up and smiled at them. "You're back! Did you two have a good afternoon?"

"The best!" Ally said, smiling. She raced into the room, quickly listing off all the things they'd seen and done.

Kate asked a bunch of questions and brought in her own experiences with each of the sites they'd visited.

"I wish you could've come with us," Ally said, yawning.

"Some other time, maybe."

Not likely.

"How did it go here for you?" he asked.

"Good."

"When will you finish?"

"Tomorrow morning. First thing."

"You're ahead of schedule."

"This clay is extremely easy to work with, so barring anything catastrophic, like something cracking as it dries, I'll only need an hour or two to finish it in the morning."

"So then we'll be leaving for Russia?" Ally asked.

He did not want to get into this tonight. "Next stop Moscow," he said, avoiding the fact that Kate and Ally wouldn't be coming with him. "Ally, I think you should head to bed." It would be best for him to go with Ally, but he needed to talk to Kate.

"I know. I'm tired. Night, Kate." She hugged Kate around the middle.

"Good night, Ally," Kate whispered.

"Night, Dad," she murmured. "I had a great day."

"Me, too." He brushed her long hair back from her face. "I'll be up in a little while to check on you."

"Okay." Her feet dragging, she left the room.

Riley listened to her footsteps as she went upstairs, down the corridor and into her bedroom before he turned back to Kate. He'd missed her today. The realization settled inside him.

"I'm glad you two spent some time together."

"Me, too." Not quite ready to address the fact of him heading to Moscow alone, he said, "So you'll really be finished with that in the morning?"

"Yep. Did you talk to March today?"

"This morning. I told him you were in the shower and he let talking to you pass."

"Because he already knew I was here."

"Exactly." He stepped closer for a better look at the progress she'd made with her statue that day. Chaos, a male god, stood on a small circular base. A rough snakelike dragon coiled at his feet. Though he held a sword above his head in his right hand, he was naked. As was typical of most Greek statues he'd ever seen, this figure's chest was smooth, broad and muscular. The hair on his head was short and curly.

"For a god of nothing and everything, a god who supposedly had no physical form, Chaos looks awfully human."

"He does, doesn't he?"

"Why is that?"

"It was part of the artist's job. To make the gods accessible to the masses."

"Are you saying this artist mass-produced these statues?"

"That's the theory. This type of statue was used as an offering by common people to the gods, so they were quite ordinary and inexpensive. It's likely why so many of this artist's figures survived."

"Then why are they so special?"

"Well, because while archaeologists have found many ancient Greek figurines through the years similar to these, these are different from the rest in one important respect. Most artists of the time didn't sign their work. This one did, in a sense. He placed a fully bloomed rosebud somewhere in each of his designs. Here on Chaos—" she pointed to the base of the statue she was working on "—the rose is on the dragon at his feet."

"So this artist was either a visionary or quite conceited."

She chuckled. "I'm going with visionary."

He glanced at the pictures she was working from. "You do amazing work."

"I needed to take a break from my own studio work, but I think I'm ready to go back. Do my own thing," she said, reaching down with a small tool to put the final touches on Chaos's privates.

"Did all gods have such small penises?" he asked.

She smiled even before glancing over at him. "I believe they did."

"So much for being a god," he muttered. "Or for that matter a goddess."

"There were other advantages."

"Like what?"

"Well, if you believe mythology, from Hesiod's perspective anyway, Chaos was responsible for all of creation. That's pretty awesome power."

"From nothing came everything?"

"Something like that. Gaia was the first to come from Chaos."

"Mother earth," Riley whispered.

"She created land, mountains and hills."

"I suppose the heavens were next."

"In some stories, yes, Uranus came next. In others it was Tartarus, creator of the underworld. Still others claim that Eros, the god of love, was second."

"That's strange."

"That from Chaos came love?"

"Yes."

"I think it's very fitting, in a way."

"That's because you've never been in love."

"No. But I imagine it to feel like a tempest. At once awful and wonderful. If that isn't chaos, I don't know what is."

It wasn't the way he'd felt toward Amy. Loving Amy had been effortless. There'd been nothing contradictory about his feelings for her. But when he looked into Kate's eyes, he knew she was right. Loving Kate would be at the same time the most awful and wonderful thing he could ever imagine.

It was exactly how he'd felt kissing her. The physical sensation of his lips on hers had been wonderful, all right. So amazing, he'd wanted more. More heat, more skin, deeper penetration. And yet more was wrong. For her. For him.

Chaos.

So if it was so bad for them both, why did he want her so desperately? "Must be why mythology is rife with tragedy."

"And joy and passion. Wonder and love. Discovery and growth."

"And incest and murder." He grinned. "Jealousy and trickery."

Silently, her gaze locked on his face, she spun around on her swivel stool, putting her eye level with his chest and only inches from him. "You have the most amazing smile and yet you so infrequently bother."

He frowned. There was no point in egging her on.

Suddenly she reached up and rested both of her hands on his chest. Then, as if he were rough clay that needed to be smoothed, she ran her palms along his pecs, down his sides and up again in a slow, circular motion. "And you have the most beautiful body. I would love to sculpt you."

As big a glutton for punishment as he'd ever known, he stood there letting her drive him crazy.

"But then you'd have to pose for me." Her fingers ran over his chest and his pebble-hard nipples. "Naked."

He groaned and grabbed her hands. "Kate—"

"Don't try to tell me you don't want this."

"Oh, I want this. More than you can imagine."

She stood with her feet still on the bottom rung of her stool, bringing herself eye level and flush against him. "Then what's the problem?" She wrapped her hands around his neck and pulled him toward her.

Their already open mouths met in a flurry of need. Warm tongues, soft lips, hot breath. He forced himself to keep his hands at his sides. If he touched her, he already knew he wasn't going to be satisfied with merely holding her. He'd want skin. Demand contact. Heat.

She hooked her foot around his leg, bringing her center closer, and with a moan he gave in, bent and wrapped his arms around her. Dragging up her T-shirt, his hands finally connected with the silky-soft skin on her back.

Before he knew it, he was the one sitting on her work stool and she'd climbed onto him, straddling him. They met, eye to eye, shoulder to shoulder, chest to…petite but oh-so-fine breasts. His groin to hers. And a hard-on pulsed uncomfortably under his jeans.

As she nibbled on his lower lip, his cell phone rang, bringing him to his senses. What was he doing? He pulled back. "I have to take this." It wasn't March's phone. This had to be Trace.

"I know," she whispered.

With one arm wrapped around Kate, he stood, set her away from him and quickly flicked on the phone. "Trace?"

"Yeah. Bad news."

Riley gripped the cell phone tighter as Trace's

tense voice sounded over the line. Jenny had to be alive. She had to still be alive. He wouldn't let himself believe anything else. "You lost March?" That had to be it.

"Outside Shanghai."

He glanced at Kate and a concerned expression flashed over her features. "Explain." He paced the floor of the workroom.

"I was hot on their tail landing in China. Met up with my men and we followed him, watching, waiting for any opening." Traced sighed. "I'm telling you, Riley, we took every precaution, but they took off in the middle of the night. Slipped away."

"Do you think he knew you were there?"

"No way. He guessed. He's being careful."

"Do you have any idea where he went?"

Kate was listening to his side of the conversation and clearly trying to make sense of it.

"Yeah," Trace said. "I can track him. Find him. Follow him." But there was something else bothering Trace. Hesitation was there in his voice.

"What else is going on, Trace? Spill it."

"This isn't going to be as easy as we thought." He paused. "March knows how you think. He knows you've called me. He's going to anticipate this move."

Probably. Riley stopped pacing. "You got a better idea?"

"Yeah." Trace paused. "I head straight to Turkey."

A chill ran along Riley's spine. "Take your sights off Jenny, and we could lose her for good."

"Riley, man, she's already out of my sight. We don't change tactics and we could lose her. The best plan of attack at this point is to jump ahead of March and set a trap for him instead of following him. If we can determine his target in Turkey, I can set up and wait for him."

"No."

"But—"

"I said no."

"Listen to me!" Trace yelled, forcing Riley to pull the phone away from his ear. "Life doesn't always happen by the book. What if March heads back to Shanghai, hops a plane and he's gone before I know it? I'd be behind him every step of the way. If we can figure out his destination in Turkey, I'll be one step ahead of him."

"March might be expecting that."

"Not from you. He expects you not to let Jenny out of sight."

Riley hated to admit it, but Trace was right.

"Let me keep one of my men tracking March. The other three of us head to Turkey. All I need to know is who his target is in Istanbul."

Kate. She knew a lot about these statues. She might know who in Turkey owned one. "Hold on,"

Riley said, glancing at Kate. He put his hand over the phone.

"What's the matter?" she said. "What happened?"

"I'll explain later. Right now I need to know if you think you can figure out who owns the last statue on March's list. The one in Turkey."

"I can try," she said.

"That's not good enough. Trace needs to know for sure."

"Riley, I can't guarantee—"

"Jenny's life depends on this."

She held his gaze. "I'll do the best I can."

Kate's best was pretty good. He put the phone back to his ear. "Trace? We'll go with your plan. Head directly to Turkey. I'll call you as soon as we know March's target."

"You sure?"

"No, I'm not sure. But Kate'll be on it. If anyone can figure this out, she can."

"Riley, I'm sorry we lost March."

"Not your fault, Trace."

Trace disconnected the call and Riley glanced at Kate. The heat of their embrace had evaporated the instant his cell had rung with Trace's call. The barest trace of regret shaded her amber eyes.

Quickly he explained what was happening with Trace. "I'm going to call it a night," he whispered, stepping away from her. "All right?"

"Sure. You go on upstairs," she said. "I'm going to stay here and make a few calls before I head to bed."

"You okay?"

"I'm fine." She turned her back on him and pulled out her cell phone.

She wasn't fine. Not even close.

But then, neither was he. With this need he felt for her building inside him, there was no way he'd be getting to sleep any time soon.

CHAPTER FIFTEEN

Friday, 12:50 a.m.

THERE. DONE. ALMOST.

Kate took a deep breath and closely examined her work one last time. Any more tweaking and she took the risk of making the clay look over-worked and ruining the rustic appeal she'd taken pains to create. Now all that was left was for the figure to partially dry to a leather-hard state so that tomorrow she could do some cutting, scraping and filing in the hopes of aging this thing several hundred years. For that final process, she'd have to wait until morning.

She took a deep breath, carefully set her work-in-progress in the middle of the counter and par-tially covered it with plastic, allowing it to dry gradually. If the clay dried too quickly, it could crack and she'd have to start all over again in the morning, but for tonight this was as good as it was going to get.

She glanced at her cell phone, saw there were messages and realized she'd unknowingly set the phone to vibrate. She'd gotten three calls back from her inquiries about the Turkish statue's whereabouts. As she listened to her voice mail, her shoulders sagged. No one had a clue who owned the statue or how to find it.

On leaving the workroom, she found the house quiet and dark, but for a dimly lit few wall sconces. Apparently everyone had long since gone to sleep. Even Riley. Although how he could've slept after that kiss they'd shared was beyond her.

She contemplated going to her room, but she was much too wired to sleep. Quietly she crept into the kitchen, snuck a couple butter cookies from the jar on the counter and then went out onto the veranda for a breath of fresh air.

Without a cloud in the sky, the almost full moon was as bright as she'd ever seen it. She went to the railing and stared out over the city of Athens, lit up and still bustling with activity even at this late hour. She could even see the Acropolis with its Christmas-tree frame now glowing with strings of blue and white lights, Greece's colors, and topped with a monstrous star.

"Hey." The soft voice sounded behind her.

Kate spun around to find Riley sitting in the shadows. "I didn't know you were out here."

"Does that mean you wouldn't be here if you'd known?"

"No. It's just…"

He stood and came toward her. "I couldn't sleep."

So their kiss had affected him more than he'd let on. "Neither of us seems to be doing much of that these days." She sighed. "I've got some bad news."

He shrugged. "I don't see how things could get much worse."

"Most of the phone calls I made tonight in trying to locate the statue in Turkey didn't pan out. No one seems to have any leads."

"We took a risk. Sometimes things go wrong."

"I'm still waiting to hear back from one art dealer. We could get lucky."

"Still planning on having the statue of Chaos finished in the morning?"

She nodded. "But it'll need more drying time before it'll be ready to fire. If it's not completely dry, inside and out, it'll explode in the kiln."

"It has to be finished before we reach Istanbul."

"That's not going to happen."

"Then what do you propose?"

"Fire it in Istanbul."

"How much firing time does it need?"

"Theoretically, at least eighteen hours. Can we get to Istanbul with that much time to spare?"

"It'll be tight, but it's possible." He looked off

into the night. "I don't know what I would've done without you, Kate."

She studied his profile. Such a proud and capable soldier. "That was hard for you to say, wasn't it?"

"I'm not used to needing people, at least not civilians."

"Well, I'm certain that even without me, you would've figured something out."

"I'm not so sure about that. I've gotten myself out of some pretty messy situations, but I've never had the life of someone I loved threatened like this."

He was trying so hard to be strong, but Kate could feel the uncertainty nearly boiling off him in waves. His big hands rested on the balcony rail. How she'd ever thought of those strong, capable fingers as beefy was beyond her. She placed her hand over his and caressed his warm skin.

His head dropped and he studied her fingers as if the look of her hand on his was too foreign to comprehend.

"I wish...things were different," she whispered. "I wish...we'd met again under different circumstances. When this is over—"

"It'll be over. We'll be over, Kate. Life goes on as before."

"You go your way, and I go mine?"

"That's what I keep trying to tell you." He pulled his hand away.

"Why does it have to be that way?"

"So many reasons I don't even know where to begin."

"Try."

"For starters, I'm twelve years older than you. Hell, I'm pushing forty. You're just getting started. You can try and argue the age difference doesn't mean anything now, but when I'm sixty, you'll only be in your mid-forties. You don't need me bogging you down."

"That sounds like an excuse to me, and a bad one at that. You're not that much older than me, Riley. Besides, I think the fact that you're older is one of the reasons we work."

He grunted.

She felt herself getting defensive. "You're more confident than any man my age. I like that. Somehow it feels right."

The man's broad chest, muscles bulging on top of muscles, and strong, square chin that said anything but gentle. Sensitive, funny, soft-spoken? Riley? Not in this lifetime. But suddenly she didn't want any of those things. Suddenly all she wanted was a hard, big man. Riley made her feel the most vibrant combination of both femininity and strength.

"What if I do want you?" She moved toward him. "What if you're exactly what I want?"

"Then I'd tell you you're crazy. Out of your mind." Instead of stepping back and away, he stood his ground.

She put her hands on his chest, felt hard muscles under her fingers and wanted more. She stared at his mouth, felt her own lips part. But he was too tall to meet face-to-face.

Wrapping her arms around his neck, she tried to pull him toward her, but he wasn't budging.

"Kate, don't do this again.…"

If he wasn't coming to her, she was going to him. She pulled herself up onto that tall frame and kissed him. Breasts pressed against his chest, she hung on him.

Any of the other men she'd dated would've been scared to death by her forwardness. Not Riley. He glanced down at her, his eyes heavy lidded, the breath puffing out of his chest. "You're starting something you're not going to want to finish."

"I'm a big girl. I can handle whatever you dish out. Try me."

He groaned out loud and, in one motion, lifted her into his arms and pinned her against the wall of the house. She swung her legs around his waist and suddenly they were face-to-face, his blue eyes intense on her face, his lips inches from hers, his arms free to explore.

"Kiss me," she whispered. "Kiss me, damn it."

He closed his eyes, buried his face in her neck and breathed in her scent. His hands traveled along her sides and settled beneath her breasts as his mouth hovered over hers. He seemed desperate to clear his head.

It took everything in her to hold back and let him make this first move. She was aching to feel his mouth on her lips, her neck. "Riley…"

Suddenly the last thread of his control seemed to snap. He pressed his lips against hers, silencing her, and his tongue slipped between her teeth as his hips pressed against her very center. He cupped her backside and held her against his erection, grinding roughly, but oh, so sweetly against her swollen flesh. If they'd been naked, she'd no doubt he'd have been inside her and she'd have been coming in seconds flat.

The small rustling noise of a lizard or squirrel sounded from the bushes, and Riley staggered back. His eyes were dark, almost black as he set her down.

A taste. That was all he was going to give her. She almost whimpered. "Riley—"

"No, Kate," he whispered. "When your head clears you'll be thanking me for ending this before it goes too far. When I leave for Moscow tomorrow, you're staying here with Angelo. Along with Ally."

"And if March asks for me when you call him?" she whispered.

"I'll make something up. He bought it this morning."

"That's because his contact saw me when we picked up supplies. March knew I was here."

"You've done more than enough already, Kate."

She touched his arms and made him turn toward her. "You're not going to want to hear this, but your battle has become mine." She ran her fingers down his cheek, resting the pad of her thumb on his mouth. "There's no going back."

He shook his head. "I can't accept that."

"You don't know how to run a kiln. You don't know how to fire that statue without ruining it. I couldn't live with myself if something happened to Jenny because of me."

Staring down at her, he said nothing.

"Jenny needs me, Riley. So do you." More than he would accept, more than he even knew.

But he couldn't argue. He knew she was right. Without a word, he was gone.

Kate leaned back against the wall and caught her breath. Her neck felt raw, her lips bruised, but she'd never felt more alive in a man's arms. All she wanted was to feel him again. And again. To what end?

Heartbreak. What else could be in store for a woman who wanted a man who refused to allow himself to want her?

RILEY CLOSED HIMSELF INSIDE the guest bedroom, leaned back against the door and jabbed his hand through his short hair. The last time he'd lost control like that with a woman he'd been all of eighteen and a virgin. After that, for years, he'd only been with Amy. Sex with her had been good, fine, though he'd always held himself back, worrying he'd hurt her. Amy had been too fragile in so many ways.

And after Amy? Come to think of it, when hadn't he held himself back with a woman?

God help him, but a woman like Amy suddenly held no appeal. He wanted a live wire in his arms. He wanted Kate. He wanted the taste of her on his tongue, her soft, eager flesh under his hands, her legs around him again. Her center swollen and wet.

He swallowed and closed his eyes.

Get a grip, soldier.

She might have argued her point well that she wanted an older man, but the fact was that she wanted babies, a family. The fire inside him died as quickly as if an ice-cold bucket of water had been dumped over his head. "I won't do that to you, Kate. Not now. Not ever."

But he was going to need Kate in Moscow, and that meant they were going to be alone. No Ally to keep them in line. Out of control was right.

"No!" ALLY ANNOUNCED in the morning, all but stomping her feet for emphasis. "I am not staying here! And you can't make me."

"Wonder where she gets that from?"

Riley glared at Kate. "You're not helping matters at all."

"Sorry." Kate sighed.

Quite early that morning she'd finished the statue. Now it was a matter of letting the clay dry completely so they could fire it in a kiln. It was time to head to the airport and on to Moscow.

Angry with Ally's childish outburst, Riley let reality sink in a bit for her and turned toward the Bebels. *"Efharistó,"* he said quietly. "Thank you, Nadi and Angelo, for everything you have done for us."

"Our home is your home. Always," Nadi said, hugging Riley. *"Adio."*

"Adio, Riley," Angelo said, shaking his hand. "Be safe."

With a worried expression, the older couple turned away. Nadi smiled at Ally. "Ally, dear. You have enjoyed your stay with us, yes?"

"Yes," Ally whispered. "But I want to be with my dad."

"I understand," Nadi said. "I want you to know that we would love to have you with us. We will have fun, too. I will teach you more Greek. Show you how to make pasteli. Honey candy. Take you shopping again."

Ally looked away.

"Okay." Nadi took Angelo's hand. "Now we'll leave you alone to discuss this." They left the living room and went into the kitchen.

The moment they were gone, Ally turned to Riley. "You said I could stay with you. You said you wanted to reconnect. It was all a lie, wasn't it?"

For the life of him, Riley didn't know how to fix this.

"Ally, honey," Kate said, pulling Ally into a big hug. "You want Jenny back, right?"

Ally nodded.

"Then you need to let your dad take care of this."

"But I can help."

"I know, honey." Kate sighed and stepped back, keeping her hands on Ally's shoulders. "But the truth is that Angelo can protect you better."

"My dad will keep me safe. I know he will."

Riley paced behind Kate.

"But if he has to worry about you, he may not be able to get Jenny back safely."

Ally glanced at Riley. "Why do you always want to get rid of me?"

"Get rid of you?" Riley stopped in front of his daughter. His anger dissipated the moment he finally understood what Ally was feeling. "Ally, that's not what I want."

"Then why do you do it?" she cried. "Every chance you get?"

Speechless, he stood there.

"Dad, I want to stay with you," Ally said stubbornly. "I'm *going* to stay with you."

All of a sudden Ally looked so much like Amy, his heart ached, but she wasn't Amy. She was her own person, and if she did take after one of her parents, it was more than likely him.

"Kate, thank you," he said. "But I need to talk to Ally myself. Alone, please."

With a soft, reassuring touch on his arm, Kate left the room.

Riley knelt in front of his daughter. "I've been wrong, Ally. Leaving you with Jenny all these years."

Ally said nothing, only looked at him with not a little bit of distrust, and he couldn't blame her.

"Jenny's been great to take such good care of you, don't get me wrong, but I'm your dad. I should be with you."

"But you've always said that wouldn't work."

"I know. And that was true. Then. But things are going to change."

"How?"

"I don't know yet." Being with Ally these past several days—and Kate—had changed things for him. "When all this is over, we'll figure it out. Somehow, some way, you and I *will* be together."

"You promise?"

"I promise." He folded his arms around her and held her tight. "Ally, honey, if anything happened to you..." He set her back and away from him. "I know you're scared. I know you want to come with me. But I need you to stay with Angelo. I need to know you're okay, so that I can focus on getting Jenny back. Okay?"

Ally's shoulders shook. "Okay."

"Listen to me." He cupped her face. "I'm coming back."

"You promise?"

"I promise." She vaulted into his arms and Riley held her as tight as he could without breaking her in pieces. "I love you, Ally."

"I love you, too, Daddy." After she'd practically squeezed the life out of his neck, she let go. "And I have to tell you something else."

"Yeah?"

"I lied about something."

He waited, wondering.

"Chocolate is my favorite cake."

"I knew it." He smiled and rubbed his thumb along her cheek. God, but he loved this little girl. Never again was he going to turn his back on her. Never again.

"Daddy, come back."

"I will."

"And take care of Kate."

"You know I will," he whispered. If necessary, with his dying breath.

CHAPTER SIXTEEN

"HAVE YOU EVER BEEN TO MOSCOW?" Kate whispered.

"Yes." Riley glanced out the window of the airplane as they made their descent to Moscow's Sheremetyevo International Airport. A blanket of white snow covered the ground as far as the eye could see. "Never in the winter, though."

The city itself, with its population of ten million plus, had long been considered Europe's largest metropolitan area, with suburbs branching out for many miles in every direction. As far as Riley was concerned, though, it looked like every other big city.

"Let me guess," she said. "On a mission."

He nodded.

"Have you been to Red Square?"

He'd been there, all right, but not in the way she meant.

"I'll bet you have," she murmured. "But you haven't really *seen* it, have you?"

"No."

"That's too bad. St. Basil's Cathedral and the

Kremlin alone are worth the trip. But there are also the museums. The famous shops." She chuckled. "The nightlife is amazing. Fabulous restaurants. Delightful theaters. Fast and furious nightclubs."

He kept his gaze focused out the window.

"We won't have time for any of it, will we?"

"No." Although this mission was nowhere near legit, it was no different than any other one. And they'd have no time to see the culture of the city. The moment Vasili Belov discovered his statues were missing he would scour the city looking for him and Kate. They had one night to get the job done and then get out of Dodge.

Kate patted her bag. "This Chaos statue needs more time to dry before firing it in a kiln."

"We'll figure it out," he said as the plane landed and taxied to the gate. Riley turned on his cell phones and checked for messages. Nothing. But then, only one of the phones March had given him looked to be working here in Russia. He glanced at Kate. "Anything from that last contact of yours on the location of the Turkish statue?"

"No," she answered after a moment. "But it's possible he e-mailed me. When we get out into the terminal, I'll check."

Purplish crescents tinged the skin under her bloodshot eyes and her voice lacked energy. After traveling to three different countries in five days, having logged more than six thousand air miles and catching sleep on planes and in cars, she looked as exhausted as he felt. All he wanted to do was squeeze her hand and tell her this would all be over soon. One way or another.

Immediately after exiting the plane, they located an internet connection. While Kate booted up the laptop Angelo had given them before leaving Athens, Riley pulled out March's cell and dialed. "I'm here," he said the moment March answered. "In Moscow."

"Put Kate on the line," March said.

He handed over the phone.

"I'm here," she said.

"Good. Then all is in order."

She handed the phone to him and went back to the laptop.

"Let me talk to Jenny," Riley said.

"She's a little…tied up at the moment."

"You bastard." He paced next to Kate. "I want to talk to her."

"And I don't want to play any more games," March said, his anger subdued but there all the same. "That's what you get for trying to double-cross me and sending your man to tail us. You're lucky I don't kill Jenny right here and now."

Riley closed his eyes for a moment and swallowed.

"Once you've secured Vasili Belov's stat-ues, head immediately to Istanbul," March said, speaking quickly. "We'll meet at 4:00 p.m. tomorrow to exchange the statues for Jenny. I'll call you with a location."

"When we were in D.C. you said I had until midnight."

"Did I? Hmmm. Things changed."

"That's too soon for me," Riley said. He had to stall. "I need more time."

"There isn't more time. The buyer is anxious to get his collection. He wants to meet at five. So you've got until four and not a moment longer."

"March—"

The man disconnected the call.

Riley turned to Kate. "Have you figured out yet who owns that last statue?"

Intent on her research, she didn't say anything.

"Kate?"

"Got it," she said. "It's a Turkish businessman." She ripped off the corner of the newspaper where she'd written down the name.

Without thinking, he planted a quick kiss on her lips before pulling out his cell phone and calling Trace. Not until he glanced back at Kate, noticing her unsettled expression, did he realize what he'd done. Kissing her had felt like the most natural thing in the world.

"Let's get through customs," he said turning away. "Find Roman and get done with this."

FOR THE FIRST TIME since this whole mess had started back in D.C. Kate was alone with Riley, and she wasn't the only one intensely aware of their proximity. From the moment they'd left Ally at Angelo's home early that morning until their six-hour flight had touched down in Russia, they'd danced around each other like skittish colts.

Her fingers would accidentally brush against his and he'd draw away from her as if she was acid. He'd touch her arm while talking or protectively rest his hand on her lower back, and she'd feel herself shift away in order to put more distance between them. Then there'd been that quick kiss. He wasn't purposely jerking her back and forth, but that's how she felt all the same. By the time they'd made their way through customs, their awareness of each other was at an all-time high.

She was actually relieved that Riley had called a friend, Roman Gordieva, while they'd still been in Athens and made arrangements to have him pick them up at the airport. Riley wanted some additional equipment and information, and Roman would likely be able to provide for everything.

"How do you know this man?" she asked as they left the customs area.

"We worked together during a peacekeeping mission in Bosnia and then met again as military liaisons in Afghanistan," he said as they moved through throngs of travelers excitedly greeting relatives and friends. "There he is." Riley pointed to a man a good thirty feet away, who was searching through the crowd. "Roman! Over here."

A man with the broadest shoulders Kate had ever seen came toward them, his arms outstretched. "James Riley," he said with a smile. Although his nose looked as if it had been broken a couple times, he was handsome, with sandy-blond hair and clear blue eyes. "I wasn't sure I would ever see you again." He grabbed Riley roughly by the shoulders and planted a quick peck on one cheek and then the other.

Smiling, Riley stepped back. "This is Kate."

"Good to meet you, Roman," she said.

"Kate. *Privyet*." He ignored her outstretched hand in favor of another set of double kisses, and then a woman stepped forward, smiling widely as she stopped next to Roman.

"This is Svetlana," Roman said. "My wife."

She was gorgeous. With a long, lanky figure, wide blue eyes and high cheekbones, she looked as if she belonged on a fashion runway in Paris.

Riley put out his hand. "Hello, Svetlana."

With tears in her eyes she pushed his hand aside and hugged him. Kate couldn't help cracking a smile as Riley threw a questioning glance at Roman, his hands still at his sides.

"What can I say?" Roman shrugged. "She's grateful you saved her ugly mug of a husband."

Clearly clueless as to what to do with this overt show of affection, Riley awkwardly patted Svetlana on the back and then pulled away. "Thanks for helping us," he said to Roman.

"Family is most important. I will do what I can to help you rescue your sister-in-law." He produced warm winter coats for both Kate and Riley before leading the way into frigid temperatures to his car outside. "So where are we going?"

"The nearest hotel," Riley said, explaining on the way that the Chaos statue needed air time. "We'll leave it in a hotel room to dry. In fact, we'll leave all of our gear there. We'll pick everything up again before we head to Istanbul."

"Then where?"

"Rublevo," Riley said. "I want to get a visual on the property."

"That area is about as exclusive as it gets." Roman glanced at him, his expression serious. "Who owns these statues you're planning to steal?"

Riley held Roman's gaze for a long moment. "Vasili Belov."

Roman shook his head. "You must be joking."

"No." Riley pulled out the file March had given him and handed it to Roman. "I have everything I need to know right here."

"Sveta, love," Roman said as they approached

his car, "will you drive so I can look at Riley's plans?"

"Of course, Romka."

Kate and Svetlana climbed into the front seat. The men climbed into the back and laid out a blueprint of Belov's estate. "March's sources indicated the statues will be here." Riley pointed to a spot on a set of blueprints. "In the study on the second floor. At the side of the house."

As Roman studied Riley's plans, Svetlana pulled up to the first hotel they found after leaving the airport.

"This will only take a few minutes," Riley said, hopping out.

While Svetlana kept the car running and Roman continued looking through Riley's files, Kate and Riley rented a room. Kate positioned the statue in such a way as to get maximum airflow for drying and cranked up the thermostat, hoping to dry the statue faster. She turned and longingly glanced at the king-size bed. "What I wouldn't give for twelve hours of sleep."

"When this is over, you can sleep all you want."

That is if they were still alive.

They climbed back into the car and Svetlana headed out to the freeway. While they cruised past the desolate winter landscape, Kate listened to the men discussing the placement of security guards and cameras.

"I have a bad feeling about this," Roman finally said. "Maybe with some additional men we could launch an assault, but sneak in, steal the statues and slip out?"

"I don't have a choice, Roman."

"You know Belov is neck-deep in organized crime?"

"I know. Did some research on him when we were in Greece."

"March too chicken to do his own dirty work?"

Riley chuckled. "If Grigori Kozmin were to find him in Russia—"

"He'd take him apart, piece by piece."

Riley nodded. "Do you know where Kozmin is?"

"Last I heard he was still in Moscow." Roman sat back. "You do realize that if Belov finds out your plans, he will not hesitate in killing you. And Kate. And if Belov finds out I helped…"

"That's why I'll be doing this alone," Riley said.

Kate glanced back at Riley, but he wouldn't look at her. Worried, she glanced at Svetlana.

"That's Belov right there," Svetlana said, indicating a photo in a newspaper sitting between the two front seats.

Kate only half heard Riley planning to keep her out of this—again—as she picked up the society pages. "Which one is he?"

"Him." Svetlana pointed at the unsmiling man in the middle.

"What's the photo about?"

Svetlana glanced at the blurb. "Apparently there is a party at Belov's estate tonight starting at eight. A fund-raiser for the Pushkin."

Although she couldn't read Russian, Kate studied the photo as Roman and Riley continued their discussion. The picture was of several people standing in front of the Pushkin Museum. She'd done some restoration work there several years back and recognized one of the curators in the picture.

"How long do we have?" Roman asked. "How long will you plan on being in Russia?"

"One night," Riley said.

"What?"

"I have to meet March in Istanbul tomorrow. Late afternoon."

"That will be a problem." Roman shook his head. "If you had a week or two to plan, you would find a way in. But with only one night?" He sounded disgusted. "I'm sorry, Riley. I don't think this can be done."

"Wait a minute," Kate muttered as a thought occurred to her. She spun around and showed the men the newspaper. "We can get into Belov's house through this fund-raiser."

Roman glanced from Kate to Riley. "But it will be an invitation-only event, and I won't be able to get you in."

"I can." Kate smiled as she tapped the paper. "I've done work for this curator at the Pushkin. Helped him out of quite a jam, in fact. He'll get us tickets."

Roman raised his eyebrows. "That's not a bad idea."

"Don't encourage her," Riley murmured.

Kate glared at him. "This can work, and you know it."

"No."

"You have a better plan?" she asked.

"I said no."

"This party at Belov's estate is our only chance."

"What I wouldn't do to attend a party at Vasili Belov's estate," Svetlana said dreamily. "For a glimpse inside that magnificent mansion."

"Never going to happen," Roman said.

"Sounds like a black-tie event, yes?" she asked her husband.

"Probably."

"What difference does it make?" Riley barked, glaring at Kate.

Ignoring him, Svetlana grinned at Kate. "I have the perfect dress for you to wear."

"I said we're not going, and that's final." Riley grabbed the paper and threw it aside. "I'll find some other way into Belov's estate."

CHAPTER SEVENTEEN

"UNBELIEVABLE," ROMAN SAID, glancing through binoculars. "That place is a fortress." His breath clouded into puffs of ice crystals in the cold air.

Riley, Kate, Roman and Svetlana were hidden inside the tree line of thick pines on the undeveloped land bordering Belov's estate, studying the comings and goings. The staff was busy with final preparations for the party, and security was tight. Every caterer's vehicle was searched inside and out. Every person entering the grounds was thoroughly patted down and IDs checked and crosschecked. Security cameras and armed guards were positioned everywhere Riley would have put them. Whoever was in charge of security knew what he was doing.

"There's got to be a way in," Riley muttered. The alternative... Well, he wasn't even going to think about it.

"Too late to nab a caterer or trade places with a guard." Roman lowered his binoculars and handed them to Kate. "Besides, you don't know Russian well enough to pass as either."

Riley could understand the language better than he could speak it.

"We don't have a choice," Kate said. "We have to go to the party as guests."

"Absolutely not," Riley said.

Svetlana raised her eyebrows at Kate.

"Why not?" Kate challenged.

"Because I won't put you at risk like that. For the last time, this isn't your battle."

"And I'm telling you for the last time," she snapped back at him, "that it sure as hell is."

"Let's get out of here." Riley marched through several inches of snow back through the woods to Roman's car. Riley had no sooner slammed his door than his cell phone rang.

"Trace?" Kate asked from the backseat.

"Yep." Holding his breath, Riley answered. "Tell me this is over."

"I wish I could." Trace sighed over the line. "We were waiting for March at the location you gave us. He showed up without Jenny."

"Your plan didn't work."

"Not exactly. But there is a positive outcome I wasn't anticipating."

"And that is?"

"March doesn't know we're here. He thinks he lost us in China."

"How do you know?"

"He's making mistakes. He's being cocky. He thinks he's got this deal nailed."

"So we have to follow this through to the end."

"I'm sorry, Riley, but it looks like it. The first chance we get, we'll get Jenny back."

Riley disconnected the call.

"It didn't work?" Kate asked.

"No."

"Which means we have no choice but to steal Belov's statues."

He nodded. *Or die trying.*

A few minutes later they were back on the freeway and heading to Roman and Svetlana's apartment to regroup. The car ride was deathly silent. Roman had initially attempted a conversation, but after no response from either Kate or Riley, he gave up. He pulled into an apartment complex parking lot.

The moment Roman stopped the car Kate hopped out and slammed the door. She paced outside waiting for Riley, her arms crossed, clearly itching for a fight.

"I'm waiting here until the coast is clear," Roman said.

"You better go out and talk to her," Svetlana whispered.

Riley climbed out of the car and faced her head-on. "I'm not discussing this anymore."

"Well, you don't get to decide. I'm going to

Belov's party and I'll steal the statues on my own if I have to." She snapped open her cell phone and dialed, presumably, the curator's number. "The only thing you get to choose," she said while waiting for the call to be answered, "is whether you're coming along as my date or my bodyguard." She stalked into the apartment complex, leaving Riley outside.

"I'll take care of her," Svetlana said. She climbed out of the car and ran after Kate.

Roman got out of the car and glanced at Riley. "She's right, you know."

Clenching his jaw, Riley looked away. "I know." But that didn't make the situation any easier to swallow.

"That's one hell of a woman. If I didn't have my Sveta, I'd be giving you a run for your money. But with you around I doubt I'd get anywhere."

Unsure as to his meaning, Riley studied the other man. Although Roman had taken himself off the playing field the moment he'd met Svetlana, the first time Riley had ever seen him, the Russian had had three women practically dripping off his arms.

"Riley, you're an idiot." Roman chuckled. "You're going to blow this, aren't you?"

KATE'S BODYGUARD. *Not again in this lifetime.*
    Date it was.

Less than an hour later, dressed in a black tux, Riley paced in Roman's kitchen waiting for Kate. His shirt collar was scratchy and his shoes stiff as a two-by-four, but there was no way he was letting her head into that party alone. He didn't want her going at all, but with Trace no closer to breaking Jenny free, Riley didn't have many options.

Antsy to get this ball rolling, he glanced at his watch. Kate and Svetlana had been sequestered in the master bedroom for the better part of the past hour, but enough was enough. He stalked through the house and knocked on the closed door. "Kate? We need to go."

"Almost ready," Svetlana answered. "She's coming."

As Kate had expected, her curator friend had guaranteed that he would get Kate's name along with a guest added to Belov's party list, so they weren't required to stop and pick up tickets. Still, Riley wanted to arrive at the estate at the peak of attendance, assuring the most distractions for Belov's security staff, and if they waited much longer the crowd was bound to thin out.

The bedroom door opened and Svetlana came out. "She's ready."

When Kate walked into the hall, it was all Riley could do to keep his jaw from flapping open. Any doubt in his mind that the teenage Kate he remembered had morphed into a grown woman was wiped away with one look at her now.

For the first time since he'd broken in to her workroom at that D.C. museum, she was wearing makeup, turning her natural beauty into dramatic splendor. Her eyes were framed with dark liner and gold shadow, and her lips were a glossy bright pink. She wore a long beaded necklace and matching earrings. Her shoulder-length hair was straight, shiny and slightly puffed up in the back with a few long bangs sweeping across her forehead. She wore a pair of sandals with the tallest heels he'd ever seen, bringing her eyes exactly level with his mouth.

But it was the dress, bloodred and cut low enough to show off some cleavage, that stunned him speechless. The skintight fabric clung to her gorgeous bottom, and the short length made her look as leggy as a newborn colt.

"You're going to freeze in that thing," he said, wishing he could get her into something…reasonable. Like a turtleneck.

"It is rather short. And tight," Svetlana said, laughing. "There's nowhere to hide a gun, that's for sure."

Nowhere to hide a gun, indeed. She'd be lucky to slide a credit card between her skin and that fabric. *Son of a bitch.* He got a hard-on looking at her.

"That's all you have to say?" Kate said, smiling and spinning around. "Come on. How do I look?"

"Nothing short of stunning," Roman said with a smile.

Kate's gaze locked with Riley's. "Well?"

"Amazing," he whispered.

"You don't look so bad yourself." She eyed him up and down. "And you shaved."

"Yeah, whatever." He ran a hand over his smooth cheek, and with monumental effort tore his eyes off Kate. "I was long overdue."

Roman's gaze heated as he glanced at his wife. "Sveta, my love, time for a new dress for you, eh? And a reason to wear it?"

"I need no reason." Svetlana grinned. "Anything for you, Romka."

Great. A lovefest. "Time for us to go," Riley said, heading for the door.

"Wait!" Svetlana said, running to a closet and dragging out a jacket-length coat in dark sable. "It's faux fur, but better than nothing."

"I can't take that," Kate said, shaking her head.

"It's okay. Roman owes me a real one, don't you, Romka?" Svetlana draped the coat over Kate's shoulders.

"That I do. One more thing before you go." Roman went to a kitchen cabinet, pulled out a full bottle of vodka and several shot glasses. He set the glasses on the table, poured out the liquor and grabbed one of the shots for himself. *"Na zdaroviye!"*

Kate picked up a glass. "Cheers!"

"Good luck tonight," Roman said.

Riley couldn't seem to take his eyes off Kate. That dress. The coat. Those legs. She glanced at him, her eyes sparkling, and his resolve spun out of focus.

Get a grip, soldier.

"Riley?" she said.

"Thank you, Roman." Unsmiling, Riley downed his shot. "Come on, Kate. Let's move."

"Showtime." Roman followed. "What kind of weapons do you need?"

"Nothing."

Kate threw a questioning gaze in Riley's direction.

"With the metal detectors," he explained, heading outside. "We won't get anything through."

Roman had managed to get hold of two vehicles for them, a sleek, shiny black Maserati and a junker with, no doubt, a big-ass engine under the hood, both of which had been stolen, since no one was taking any chances that what happened tonight might be traced back to Roman.

"You take the Maserati," Riley said to Kate as he walked toward the getaway car.

"Be careful," Roman said.

"Come back someday for a real visit," Svetlana said. "Both of you."

"Thanks for everything," Riley said, glancing at the couple. "If there's ever anything I can help you with…"

"I know, Riley. I know." Roman gave him a quick, tight man-hug. "As soon as you have the statues, you two must leave Moscow immediately."

"Understood." Belov was so well connected it would likely take him only a few hours after finding out his statues were gone to identify Riley and Kate. "I'll let you know when we hit Istanbul."

"Do svidanye," Roman said.

Riley glanced at Kate. "You ready?"

She nodded.

"Let's do this."

Their journey to the ultraposh suburb of Rublevo west of Moscow was uneventful. Once they drew near the grounds of the Belov estate, Riley pulled off to the side of the road. Kate followed, letting the car idle while he hid his car in the woods.

A moment later he joined Kate in the Maserati. As they approached the mansion, lit up in full splendor for the fundraising event, Kate said, "I have to admit I'm a little nervous."

"Stick to the plan and you'll be fine. Act naturally and visit with your curator friend. He's bound to introduce you to others. As soon as you're settled with his group, I'll slip away to take care of getting the statues. Give me ten minutes max, then you leave alone in the Maserati. As soon as I have the statues, I'll slip out through the grounds, take the other car and meet you at the hotel by the airport."

"Piece of cake," she said lightly as they waited in line for a valet to take their car.

Right. She was at risk, they both knew it, and it didn't sit well with Riley. If any of Belov's security people discovered what Riley was up to, it wouldn't take them long to view security camera footage and identify Kate as his associate. Riley had been heavily trained for much riskier assignments than this, but Kate? If they got caught on this one, there was no going to prison. Belov would simply execute them. That is, if they were lucky.

Over and over again in the past couple of days, opportunities had presented themselves for her to bow out of this mess. She could have, probably should have, left him high and dry. He wouldn't have blamed her. She'd never even fired a gun. But over and over again she'd chosen to stay and help.

"Why?" he whispered into the quiet darkness of the car.

She turned toward him. "Why what?"

They were only a couple cars away from the front entrance. She could still back out. "You don't have to do this, you know," Riley said. "You don't need to be a part of this."

"Yes, I do."

"March isn't your problem. Any number of times these past few days, you could've left. Walked away. No one would've blamed you. I'd understand. So why are you helping me?"

"It's the quickest way for you to get the statues."

That he couldn't argue.

"Kinda kills you that you've needed me on more than one occasion, doesn't it, Riley?"

In spite of himself and the inherent danger they faced, he chuckled.

"Seriously, though." She glanced into his eyes. "You're not as bulletproof as you think."

He knew. Being around Kate—and Ally— seemed to be making him even more aware of his vulnerabilities. Unfortunately, tonight that presented a problem. If they were to achieve their objective, he had to stay as focused as a machine, and that was going to prove hard to do with her in that dress.

CHAPTER EIGHTEEN

UNDER A BRIGHT FULL MOON, Kate climbed out of the Maserati. The air was crisp and cold. Small, airy flakes of snow fell miraculously from the clear sky, as if magic drifted in the air. Riley came to her side and handed the car keys to a valet. A moment later a security guard located Kate's name on the guest list, and without a hitch they were directed straight into the foyer of the traditional, Tudor-style mansion. The party was already in full swing as an attendant took Svetlana's fur jacket from Kate.

Moving through the throngs of guests, a thrill of anticipation running along her spine, Kate watched for Sasha. She would've been lying to say she wasn't, at least in part, enjoying this night's promise of intrigue, not to mention the fanfare and decorations. She'd never been to this extravagant a private party.

"Have you ever seen anything quite like this?" she asked Riley as they were making their way through the crowd.

"Never," he murmured.

A Christmas tree, at least twelve feet tall and lavishly decorated, stood sentinel in a far corner. Lights had been strung like a loosely knit spider-web over the crowd. A sweeping staircase far off to the right was decorated with red satin bows and aromatic pine garlands. And the backdrop for all this finery consisted of the largest windows Kate had ever seen in a private home. It was black outside, but the full moon shone brightly through the glass, illuminating the light, fluffy snow continuing to fall. The setting was nothing short of enchanting, and if the never-ending flutes of champagne, trays of extravagant appetizers, and diamonds dripping off the women guests were any indication, Moscow's wealthiest were in attendance.

"Did you know that a good chunk of the world's billionaires live in Moscow?" she whispered over the sounds of a live band playing soft, classical jazz.

"I did."

"No one seems to know where they got all their money."

"That's easy," he whispered in her ear, sending a shot of awareness low in her belly. "Some are in the illegal oil trade. Smuggling weapons. Not to mention drugs and human trafficking. If it's illegal, organized crime is into it."

She glanced over at him and it was as if she was seeing Riley for the first time. For a soldier, he looked awfully comfortable in this setting and in a tuxedo. As much as she enjoyed him dressed down in a T-shirt and worn jeans, she liked the looks of him clean shaven and dressed to kill.

"Do you see him anywhere?" he asked.

"Who?" She stared at that rugged cleft in his chin, more visible now that he'd shaved.

"Sasha," he said, studying her with a critical eye. Then he gently patted her cheek. "Kate, where are you? Focus."

"Right."

He held her arm, his face serious. "This isn't a game, Kate. Everything you see around here is for show. Vasili Belov is not a nice man. He's linked to one of the most ruthless crime syndicates in the world. You need to be at the top of your game tonight. Okay?"

"You're right. I know." Reorienting herself, she took a deep breath.

As if to prove his point, Kate suddenly became aware of the one incongruent piece to an otherwise perfect picture—the smell of cigarettes and the slight haze of smoke hanging in the air. At least one person in every group had a cigarette dangling from his or her hand and there were ashtrays, nearly filled with butts, on every flat surface. She wasn't in D.C. anymore.

Turning her attention back to the crowd, she scanned faces for her friend. The security guards stationed at every corner of the patio and inter-spersed along the edges of the yard snapped her back to attention the way nothing else could. A moment later she spotted Sasha with a small group of people standing near a bubbling water fountain next to the dance floor.

He grinned and waved her over.

"Sasha!"

"Kate! *Privyet!*"

"It's such a welcome surprise to see you again." He hugged her. "I'm so happy you called." He introduced her to the others in his group, all coworkers.

Kate introduced Riley as her traveling compan-ion, and the conversation went from there, as Sasha and his friends all spoke at least some English. What do you do? How long are you in Russia? Where are you staying? And on and on while couples danced nearby on the crowded floor.

Waiters carried around trays of ice-cold cham-pagne and martinis. Also offered were various appetizers—caviar blini, smoked herring, stuffed mushrooms, a variety of shish kebabs and trays of fresh fruit, including every type of melon you could imagine. Desserts of honey cakes and choco-late sponge cake were offered, as well.

Too nervous to eat, Kate didn't touch a thing. Al-though Riley had snatched a martini from a pass-ing waiter, he didn't take a sip. Finally he set the glass down and whispered in her ear, "It's almost time." He held out a hand. "Dance with me?" His soft commanding voice tripped through her like a shot of electricity.

Without a word, she put her hand in his and they slipped seamlessly onto the dance floor. Moving in slow, sensuous rhythm, Riley pulled her close. She rested her cheek on his chest, felt his heat through the crisp dress shirt and wished she could transport them to another place, another time, where Jenny was safe and March was out of the picture.

Suddenly he stopped moving, his embrace tightened around her and Kate held her breath. So much had happened between them in such a short amount of time, she didn't know where to begin piecing it all together. Only one thing was for sure. She could love this man, was already loving him.

"Kate," he whispered. "I…"

She drew back and glanced into his face. *Say it, Riley. I know you're feeling this, too.*

He held her gaze for a moment, looked as if he might spill his guts and then, instead, leaned forward and planted a soft kiss on her forehead. "I need to go." As if he couldn't get off the dance floor fast enough, he drew her back to Sasha's group. "That's Vasili Belov, isn't it?" he asked Sasha. "Up there by the Christmas tree?"

Sasha turned. "*Da.* That's him."

"And the woman in white next to him?"

A platinum blonde with long flowing hair and glittering jewelry, she was one of the more stunning people at the fund-raiser. The only thing spoiling her look was her extremely bored expression.

"His wife," he answered.

Belov, on the other hand, distinguished-looking with salt-and-pepper hair, didn't look bored as much as watchful, as if he expected something to go wrong at any moment.

Kate glanced at Riley and found him assessing not only Belov, but also the security guards, ready to make his move. Smiling, clearly for the benefit of those around them, he leaned toward her and whispered, "This is it."

"Be careful," she whispered back.

Despite the curve to his lips, the look in his eyes was intense and serious as he squeezed her arm. "Don't wait around. I mean it, Kate. The sooner you get out of here, the better."

Suddenly their plan seemed more than flawed. It seemed impossible. "I'm worried about leaving you."

"Don't be. This is what I do." He touched her cheek in a surprisingly tender gesture and his gaze moved to her lips. For a moment she could've sworn he was going to kiss her. "In ten minutes, tell Sasha you're not feeling well and leave. Make sure you're not followed. Okay?"

She nodded.

"Promise me you'll leave."

Glancing into his eyes, she suddenly wanted to promise so much more to him.

"Kate."

"I promise. Ten minutes."

Slowly he slipped into the crowd and never looked back.

RILEY WAS IN BIG TROUBLE, and it didn't have a thing to do with March or Vasili Belov. His feelings for Kate were becoming a lot more serious than simply wanting to get her in bed with him. Complicated. He hated complicated. As he walked away from her, it took everything he had in him to not look back.

Focus. All she has to do is walk back out to the car and leave. She'd do it. He knew she would.

Riley made his way through the crowd. The information March had provided indicated the statues were displayed in Belov's library on the second floor. Even without a guard stationed at the base of the main staircase near the main entrance, that route wasn't an option. The steps were too open, too visible to the crowd below.

Based on the blueprints of the home, he thought his best bet was a staircase off the kitchen. All he had to do was get past the security guard stationed at the double doors the catering staff was using to access the kitchen. Ten minutes upstairs. That's all he needed.

He snatched a nearby tray partially filled with dirty plates and glasses, lifted it above his head and quickly covered the remaining fifty feet. As he approached the security guard near the doors leading into the kitchen, he stumbled, tipping the tray and sending a plate of stuffed mushrooms flying. Several hit the guard in the chest.

"Idiot!" the guard hissed in Russian, grabbing a napkin and dabbing at the grease stains on his white shirt.

Riley put his head down, mumbled an apology and slipped through the doors. Immediately he stopped in the shadows to assess the situation. Through the catering staff's frenzied activity, he located the steps leading to the second floor. A security guard was stationed at the base.

He put the tray on the floor, grabbed an empty martini glass and walked toward the guard, weaving a bit as he went. "Where's the bathroom…in this joint?" he said, slurring his words. As he came closer to the guard, he threw an arm over the man's shoulder and slumped into him. "Someone said I c…could take a pi…iss back here."

The guard grabbed Riley around the waist as he said something in Russian into his earpiece. Then he took a step toward the back service entrance, dragging Riley with him. "Sir, I'm going to escort you outside," he said in stilted, accented English. "Please come with me."

Doing his best to remain limp, Riley glanced around. A few of the catering staff had watched the goings-on for a moment, but were now all back to work. This wasn't perfect, but it would have to do.

The moment they hit the cold outside air, Riley slipped behind the guard, wrapped his arm around his neck in a sleeper hold and after a brief struggle immobilized him. He stashed his body behind a row of bushes, grabbed the man's gun and earpiece in hopes of keeping tabs on what was happening with security and went back inside, slipping up the stairs.

The lights were off on the second floor. Not wasting any time, he located the library at the other end of the house. Penlight in hand and mundane chatter sounding over the earpiece, he located a display of original works of art front and center in the room. Kate had described exactly what to look for and he was able to quickly identify the statues March wanted, rosebuds carved on both. Taking the statues, though, would leave a large open spot on the shelving. Someone coming into the room might very well notice the missing artifacts before he and Kate had time to leave. A couple paperweights on the desk of the approximate shape and size of the statues caught his eye.

Footsteps sounded out in the hall.

"I'm not sure where he went," one of the guards said over his earpiece line. Riley might not have been fluent in the language, but at least he could understand most of what was being said. "A waiter said one minute he was standing at the steps in the kitchen. The next minute he was gone."

They were looking for the guard or Riley. Possibly both. Quickly he snatched the statues, shoved them into a small pack and set the paperweights in the case.

"Alert," called out one of the guards over the line. "We have an intruder in the house."

They were looking for Riley. This security team was fast.

The door to the library opened as Riley slipped into the adjoining bedroom. On opening the closet, which was a room in and of itself, he moved behind the door and waited. For the moment he was stuck here.

Whoever had entered the library was now checking out the bedroom. As soon as all was quiet, he could slip out the window on the far side of the house and make a run for the car.

Footsteps sounded in the bathroom and he held his breath.

"The security tapes show the man arriving with a woman in a red dress," someone said over the line. "Find her."

Now they were after Kate. He glanced at his watch. Only eight minutes since he'd left her. What were the chances she'd headed for the Maserati early?

KATE ONLY HALF LISTENED to the heated conversation Sasha was having with his friend about a contemporary Russian painter's style or lack thereof. She glanced at her cell phone. Riley had disappeared into the crowd a little less than ten minutes ago. Since then, the perfect opportunity hadn't presented itself for her to beg illness and leave. But Riley was right. There was no point in her being here.

"Sasha?" she interrupted, touching his arm.

Startled, he spun toward her. "Yes, Kate?"

"I'm sorry. I so appreciate you clearing the way for me to come tonight, but I'm not feeling—"

"Excuse me, miss?" The man's voice came from behind her.

She turned to find a security guard assessing her, and her heart nearly lodged in her throat. Had they caught Riley? "Yes," she said breathless.

"*Puzhalasta*. Come with me. Please?" As he reached out to place his hand at the small of her back, his suit jacket swung out, revealing a gun holstered at his side.

Something was wrong. It was there in his eyes,

a look as impassive as stone. "To where?" she asked.

"This way." His hand lightly directed her toward the stairs. "Mr. Belov would like to meet you."

She glanced toward the steps and found Belov watching her, his expression even less readable than the guard's.

Sasha smiled at her. "Go on, Kate. We'll wait here for you."

"Why would he want to—"

"Please. Come." The man's grip turned painful as he squeezed her side.

All Kate could think about was Riley, and a burst of panic rushed through her body. Roman had made it very clear what Belov would do to them if he discovered their intentions. This was as real as it got.

CHAPTER NINETEEN

ALL WAS QUIET. SECURITY apparently felt they'd cleared this end of the mansion. Riley slung his pack holding the statues over his shoulder, stepped out of the closet and swiftly made his way to the balcony. As he opened the door to the outside, where he'd planned to climb a trellis down to the ground and go on to the car hidden in the woods, loud voices sounded behind him in the library.

"Sit down. Now tell me. Where is the man who came with you tonight?"

"I don't know."

Kate! They had her. Riley crept quietly along the balcony to the library doors and peered through the glass. Vasili Belov stood in the middle of the room. Directly in front of him was Kate, her hands tied behind a chair. Riley ducked back out of sight. Then a slap sounded from the room. Belov had hit her. It was all Riley could do to hold himself back.

Think. Think!

"I'll ask again," Belov said. "Where is the man you were with?"

"I told you," she said. "I don't know."

"Why are you here? What do you want?" He slapped her again. "Start talking, woman, or you will not walk away from this alive."

"Mr. Belov," a guard said, coming into the room, "Sikorski has come around. He can talk now."

The guard Riley had knocked out and left outside.

"I'll be back in five minutes," Belov said in Russian. "Get her ready to talk."

Riley glanced through the glass. Only one guard was in the room with Kate and he was moving toward her. This was the only chance Riley was going to get. He went back into the bedroom and charged into the library. The man was leaning over Kate. The instant he heard Riley, he straightened. Reached for his weapon. Riley tackled the man, grabbed his gun and smacked him on the side of the head with it, knocking him out.

"Quick. Let's go. Out the balcony." He untied Kate. "When we get outside, not a sound, keep to the shadows. We'll be out of this in two minutes."

They raced through the library's French doors.

"Down the trellis," he whispered, going first. The moment he hit the snow-covered ground he looked up. Kate was moving, but not fast enough. "Jump, Kate. I'll catch you."

She surprised him by doing exactly as he asked

and falling into his arms. He set her down and she stumbled on the icy cobblestone path surrounding the house. Those damned high-heeled sandals. Holding her hand, he ran with her across the moonlit yard through the snow and into the woods. In seconds they'd made it to the line of birch, oak and evergreens, but there were guards already coming around the corner of the house.

Riley grabbed Kate's arm and held her back behind the cover of a large oak tree. "Shh." He put his finger to his lips. "We need to move slowly, so they don't hear us."

"Did you get the statues?"

"Yes." He showed her his pack.

She shivered as snowflakes landed on her bare shoulders. "You should've left without me."

Less than a week ago that's exactly what he would've done. But today? "Never," he whispered. Her cheeks were red and swollen from Belov striking her. He smoothed his hand lightly over her bruising skin, trying to tell her with one look everything he was feeling and thinking. But now wasn't the time or the place.

He glanced back to see the guards crossing the yard. The only sound was the whoosh of Kate's breath and Riley's own heartbeat thundering in his ears. Until one of the guards stopped and said something Riley couldn't hear to one of the other men. They both glanced toward the woods.

Their footprints in the snow. Damn it. There wasn't a chance they were both going to make it out of this alive, and he refused to let anything happen to Kate.

"Kate, you need to go," he whispered, handing her the keys. "Now. Head straight through the woods. About a hundred yards. Find the car where we left it not far from the road. If I'm not with you in five minutes, leave."

"No."

"Kate—"

"I said no," she whispered fiercely. "I'm not leaving you again."

He knew that stubborn set to her mouth. There was nothing he could say or do to get her to change her mind. The guards were getting closer.

"Cover the grounds! And those woods!" a man called from near the house. "Find that man."

That voice. Riley knew that voice. His thoughts raced a mile a minute. This could be the best thing that had ever happened to him. Or his worst nightmare. "Kate, I have to go back."

"Are you out of your mind? For what?"

"I don't have time to explain." He gripped her shoulders. "Please. Go to the car and wait."

"No."

No more time to argue. "Fine." He led her to a spot behind a group of trees. Then he took off his jacket and wrapped it around her. "If things go badly for me, *then* you have to leave. Understand me?"

"I can help—"

"Kate, listen." He gripped her shoulders. "I need you to do this for me." He admitted it. Freely. To himself. To her. He needed her. "I don't know if this is going to work, but if I've miscalculated I need you to take care of Ally. Please. If I don't come back in ten minutes, forget about the statues. Get to the airport and get on the first plane to Athens."

He could see her wavering. Ally. Mentioning her was what did it.

"Unless I give you an all clear, don't come after me. No matter what you hear or see happening to me out there. Understand?"

Tears puddled in her eyes and spilled down her cheeks. "You came after me."

He kissed her. Hard and fast. "Kate, you're the strongest woman I've ever known. But you're not trained for this, and the two guns I took from the guards are not enough firepower. If I don't come back, go to the car. For Ally's sake. And mine. Because I can't stomach the thought of you getting hurt."

"For Ally." She swallowed. "All right." Still the tears kept coming.

"Get down. In the middle of these evergreens. Stay here."

Riley turned and headed into the clearing. It was going to be a long time before he could wipe the image of Kate's tear-streaked face from his memory. He walked out of the woods and toward the guards, hoping this wasn't the biggest mistake of his life.

"Stoi!" one of the guards called. "Stop!"

The other security guards near the house spun around, their guns drawn.

Riley put his hands in the air. "Grigori Kozmin? Where are you?"

"Who wants to know?" answered the man nearest to Riley. It wasn't Kozmin.

"I have some information he's going to want."

One of the other men came toward Riley, and Riley held his breath. What if it wasn't Kozmin? What if he'd been wrong?

"James Riley," the man finally said.

Riley released his breath. "Hello, Grigori."

Kozmin's fist came out of nowhere, slamming into Riley's gut like a sledgehammer and knocking the wind out of him. Riley's every instinct had him wanting to fight back, to protect himself and Kate. But he couldn't. Not yet.

"Give me one reason why I shouldn't kill you." Kozmin stepped back and aimed his gun at Riley's heart. "Right here. Right now."

"Because I was telling you the truth back in that

bar in Georgia. I didn't know it was March you were beating to a pulp."

"So you claim."

"If you kill me, then you wouldn't hear what I have to say, and that would be a shame."

"Maybe. Maybe not."

"Trust me. This you're going to want to hear."

"RILEY!" Kate placed her hand over her mouth to stifle a cry as one of the guards punched him. It was all she could do not to call out or run to him. But without a weapon she'd accomplish absolutely nothing.

Ally. She had to think of Ally.

She couldn't hear a word they were saying as they pointed their weapons at Riley and directed him toward the house. That's when she realized he still had the statues with him, in his pack. What was he up to? Quickly she glanced at her cell phone.

Three minutes ticked by, every second passing as slowly as an hour. *Oh, God. Oh, God. Oh, God.* If anything happened to Riley, she didn't know how she could deal with it. In these few short days he'd come to mean more to her than any man she'd ever known.

Five minutes.

Get your ass out here, Riley. I will leave. I swear to God I will.

Eight. Her breath clouded in the cold air and she shivered.

I'm walking toward the car.

Nine.

Now.

Ten.

I mean it.

He didn't come. No one did.

She pulled his tux jacket more tightly around her and breathed in his scent clinging to the fabric. *Riley.* She had no weapon, nothing to take down any of the guards. Even if she did somehow manage to tackle one of the guards and snatch his gun, she'd take down another one, maybe two guards before they killed her.

Ally. Oh, baby.

Kate dropped back to the ground and put her face in her hands, trying to think of something. Anything. As several more long minutes passed, her feet and hands all but frozen from the cold, all the remaining hope she had of every seeing Riley alive again dimmed and then completely fizzled out.

That's when the truth settled inside her. James Riley didn't walk away from responsibility. He did what he thought was best for the people he loved, even at great expense to himself. The way he'd let Jenny raise Ally. The way he'd do anything to save Jenny. The way he'd walked back to Belov's mansion.

Riley wasn't her father. He wasn't going to leave her when all this was over because he didn't care. He was going to leave her because he thought it was the best thing for her.

But he was wrong. Life was never going to be the same again. He'd given her a glimpse of what could be, put it within her grasp and then yanked it away.

When a branch snapped in front of her, she glanced up. "Riley," she whispered.

He was standing there as big and strong and alive as ever. And all alone. "You were supposed to leave."

"You're alive," she whispered as relief and a new round of uncontrollable shivers surged through her. She pushed through the branches of the pine trees and ran to him, wrapped her arms around his waist and held on, never wanting to let go ever again. This time, with this man, there was no going back.

He pulled away. "We have to go." Grabbing her hand, he turned. His pack was gone.

"Where are the statues?"

"Kozmin has them."

"Grigori Kozmin?"

"He's Belov's chief of security."

"But what? Why?"

"It'll be all right, Kate." He drew her toward where they'd hidden the other car. "Let's get out of here before Kozmin changes his mind."

CHAPTER TWENTY

"COME ON. We've got to get you warm," Riley said, drawing a still-shivering Kate out of the car.

She was barefoot, those ridiculous stiletto heels long since ruined in their race to get away from Belov's estate. Lifting her in his arms, he carried her across the icy parking lot. They'd driven straight from Rublevo to their hotel near the airport.

The moment Riley opened the door a blast of hot air hit him in the face. It was a good thing they'd cranked up the heat before heading to Roman's. The warmth would be exactly what she'd need after all that time in the woods.

He set her down, replaced his tux jacket still draped over her bare shoulders with a warm blanket from the closet and drew it tight around her.

"Why did you give him back the statues?" she asked, her teeth chattering.

"Kozmin wants March," Riley explained. "I suggested he come to Istanbul and settle his score."

"That's a big risk."

"Yeah, I know. Is the clay dry yet?"

"Not completely," Kate said. Thank goodness she'd finally stopped shivering.

He took off his tie, flung it onto the bed and undid several buttons on his shirt. "Will it be ready to fire by the time we get to Istanbul?"

"It's possible."

He glanced around the room. They had some time before they needed to be at the airport for their flight to Turkey. "We might as well get some rest."

Although, he had to admit that as wired as he was, the chances of him actually sleeping were zero to none. Not to mention this situation was danger times ten, given the room they'd rented, which had only one king-size bed. They could have gotten another room, but he didn't trust Kozmin not to go back on his word and come after them, so there was no way he was letting Kate out of his sight until the meeting with March in Turkey.

"I'm not sure I can sleep," she whispered, her voice catching.

He glanced back and froze at the sight of her. How could he have missed it? She was literally falling apart at the seams.

The red dress she wore puckered on one side where it had ripped. The stretchy fabric that had once been as smooth as silk was now dotted with snags from sliding down the trellis at Belov's estate or hiding in the pine trees in the woods. Her once smooth, creamy legs and arms were now marred with dirt and scratches. Her hair, matted and knotted, went every which way. Her lipstick had long since worn off and mascara smudged the undersides of her eyes. A slight bruise had formed on the left side of her face, courtesy of Belov, and a trail of dried tears stained her cheeks. With the light of the full moon streaming through the window hitting her in profile, she looked—for the first time ever—fragile.

"Back at Belov's. In the woods," she whispered. "I thought…you were dead."

"Shh, Kate." Slowly he closed the distance between them and wrapped his arms around her. She was shaking, quite likely from shock, as it was too hot in this room for anyone to be cold. "It's okay. We're both okay."

He dropped into the chair with her in his lap and for a long while he held her, running his fingers through her hair and his hands along her arms. Finally her trembling subsided and her muscles relaxed.

"Maybe a shower would do you some good," he whispered, plucking the fragment of a dried leaf from her hair.

"I don't want to move."

"All right, then. Hold on. I'll be right back."

He slipped out from under her, went into the bathroom and came back with several steamy washcloths and the hotel ice bucket filled with hot soapy water. Then he knelt before her, laid one warm and moist cloth on the scrape on her right knee and went about gently cleaning her legs and feet. Then he poured more clean, hot water, grabbed another fresh cloth and started in on her arms. He moved up her neck and on to her face. She surprised him by silently allowing him to pamper her. Gently he wiped away the mascara, the dirt smudges, the tearstains. By the time he reached her lips, she was a pool of jelly.

"All better?" he whispered, sitting back.

"That's the nicest thing anyone has ever done for me." Her eyes turned bright. "Riley—"

He kissed her, slanted his mouth over hers and took her breath, her soul, into him, and a sense of contentedness, the likes of which he'd never felt before, suffused him.

She pulled back, looked deeply into his eyes and asked, "What if Amy had lived?"

"What do you mean?"

"Would you have stayed in the military?"

He'd never considered it. What was the point? She'd died and he'd made his decisions. That was that. "I don't know."

"Do you think you would've done anything different with your life?"

"Kate, I have no clue."

"Would you have gone back to D.C., gotten a

regular Joe Schmo job and had a couple more kids?"

"What difference does it make?"

"I'm not sure. But there are some things about you that aren't adding up."

He shouldn't ask. He should let it go, but a part of him was curious. "Like what?"

"Like you leaving Ally with Jenny. You say it was because you didn't trust the kind of father you'd have been, but I've seen you with her. You're a good dad. You didn't abandon Ally the way my father abandoned me. You're the kind of person who doesn't take responsibility lightly. You do the right thing all the time. So how is it you've been able to sleep at night knowing someone else is raising your daughter?"

"That's none of your business."

"You know what I think?"

"No. And I don't want to know. But I'm going to guess that's not going to stop you from telling me."

"I think you would've died ten times over if you could've saved Amy's life."

He would have, too. How many times had he wished it had been him? As much as he'd put himself at risk through the years, it should've been.

"I think her death broke your heart."

He stared at her. *Don't go there, Kate.*

"I think you're scared of putting your heart on the line again. And you don't even know it."

"That's ridiculous—"

"I never figured you for such a pansy." She leaned forward and kissed him.

"So now I'm a pansy?"

"Yeah. A hulking. Muscle-bound. Wuss," she whispered against his lips. "And now it's my turn to pamper you."

"No," he murmured, standing. "That wasn't my intention."

"Well, it is mine." Purposefully she stepped toward him. Then her fingers were at the buttons on his shirt, making short order of them. In seconds her hands were on his bare chest, then on his shoulders as she dragged off his shirt. She slipped behind him, pushed him facedown onto the bed, and began to deeply massage his back, his shoulders and his arms.

Her hands felt like heaven on his skin, but it wasn't close to what he really wanted from her. It was all he could do not to turn and take her right then and there.

"I'm not that kid you have locked in your memory, Riley," she whispered, her warm hands sliding over his back. "I'm a woman. I know what I want."

"That's the problem." He flipped over and grabbed her hands, disengaging from her touch so that he could think. "You want a man who can settle down with you. Make a home together and build a family. A man who can promise to be with you tomorrow and every day afterward."

"Are you suggesting there's something wrong with that?"

"Not for a minute. But that man is definitely not me."

"How can you be so sure?" Pulling her hands out of his grasp, she sat back, unbuckled his belt and unzipped his trousers.

"Don't, Kate." He grabbed her hands again. "You need to understand." He had to do this for her sake. Her eyes had to be wide open. "You want a storybook life. And there is nothing about me that's by the book."

"You want a home and a family as much as I do. I know you do. Don't lie to me."

"A man can want something he doesn't have a right to. In my heart I'm still a soldier. That's never going to change."

"This doesn't have anything to do with you being a soldier." She stood and yanked off his pants. "At least have the balls to admit it."

He sat up. Dressed only in his boxers, he silently held her gaze. "I think you'd better explain that."

"Okay. How's this? For all that brawn and bravado you tote around like armor, you're still just scared. Scared you can't control your world. Scared that people you love will be hurt and you won't be able to stop it. Scared of feeling helpless. You hate feeling helpless, don't you, Riley? Like this situation with March."

Helpless was exactly how he'd felt. For days.

"And helpless is exactly how you felt after Amy died," she went on. "Trying to take care of a little baby all on your own. That's really why you left Ally with Jenny, isn't it? You were scared. Scared bad things would happen to Ally if you didn't."

She'd made a lot of damned good points, but there was no way he was about to acknowledge that. "So what if you're right about me?" he whispered. "That doesn't change the fact I'm not the man you need."

"Maybe you are. Maybe you aren't." She pushed him back onto the bed. "But you're definitely the one I want."

Ready to push him to the edge of the world and back again, she reached toward her side, unzipped her dress and let it fall to the ground. A condom packet was stuck to the skin under her arm, along with a credit card. The dress had been tight, but not too tight for a few necessities.

But it was the sight of her tattoo, that cluster of little blue butterflies stretching from under her left breast back along her side, like a swarm, that turned his throat dust-dry.

"Remember me?" she whispered.

He groaned, wanting to touch her so badly he could taste her. How was he supposed to think enough to resist, with her standing before him wearing no bra and only the skimpiest red thong? But then, that was her point, wasn't it?

She climbed on top of him and kissed him.

Her mouth was hot and insistent. From the first moment he'd met her all those years ago, if he was honest with himself, this was what he'd wanted from her. How was he supposed to take the high road and hold back? "Kate," he whispered against her lips, giving her—and himself—one last chance to back out. "Don't do this."

She sat back, putting her sweet center over his erection. "You'll have to stop me." She pressed her mouth against his neck, left a trail of kisses across his chest and lower on his stomach. "Push me away, Riley. I dare you."

She went lower. Lower still, dragging his boxers off as she went. Then her mouth was on his erection, her fingers tightening around the base, and he jerked with pleasure or pain, he wasn't entirely sure. "Kate, I'm warning you," he breathed.

"Consider me fully warned." Her breath buffeted his wet skin as she flicked the head of his penis with her tongue.

When her mouth closed over him again, the last of his control snapped. He buried his fingers in her hair, gripped her shoulders and pulled her up to him. He kissed her, holding nothing back.

She pulsed against him, sliding swollen, luxurious wetness up and down his shaft. He grabbed her hips, holding her still a moment, poising himself at her center. Then he pulled her down onto him, thrusting completely inside her, and she whimpered.

He grabbed the mattress and froze, holding himself back. "I'm sorry," he breathed through his clenched teeth.

"Sorry? Are you crazy? You feel amazing." She pulsed down on him.

Softly he cupped her breasts, ran his hands along every one of those tiny butterflies and kissed her deeply. Then he took in the sight of her. The image of her above him, her hips moving over him. Riley had never seen anything more beautiful in his life. Until she orgasmed around him, her face overcome with release.

He could've let go in that second and joined her, but that wouldn't have been perfect, and perfect is what he knew sex with Kate could be. He waited until she'd completely had her way with him, ridden out her last wave and collapsed on top of him.

Then he moved again, slowly, deeply, holding her hips against him as he pulsed in and out of her. She groaned against his mouth, but he wouldn't let her move. Her heartbeat thudded faster and faster. She shuddered against him, coming again.

He chuckled. "Is it always like this with you?"

"No. Never," she breathed, kissing him. "It's you, Riley. It's you."

Knowing that he couldn't hold back any longer, he needed to feel her under him. Rolling them both over, he covered her, carefully supporting the bulk of his weight so as not to crush her. He moved inside her, thrusting into her over and over. This was what he'd wanted, needed to feel.

"No." She wrapped her legs around him, pulling him down. "I want to feel all of you. Your weight, Riley. On me. Over me. I want all of you. Everything you've got to give."

With Amy, he'd always held a part of himself back, afraid he'd scare or hurt her. With every woman since, he'd always felt too big and too rough to let go. "Kate—"

"Please."

Slowly he lowered his full weight onto her. She tilted her hips, giving him the deepest access to her, and once he started pulsing into her, he didn't want to—couldn't—stop. This was, indeed, as perfect as he'd expected. He felt the last of his control slip. A piece of him broke free as he let go, thrusting into her with everything he had, nothing held back, no restraint.

"Oh, Kate," he groaned. "Kate!" This time

he joined in her release, a release that seemed to never want to end. When he thought it might be too much, his body shuddered one last time. Slowly he collapsed on top of her, burying his face in her neck.

"Now I can die," she whispered.

"What?" He glanced into her eyes.

She tilted her head and kissed him, rubbed her nose against his neck. "It can't get any better than that."

She might be right. Then again, what had just happened might very well have been only the beginning of how things could be between them. *But you'll never know, Riley. For Kate's sake, this is never happening again.*

As soon as the thought entered his mind, he knew she was 100-percent right about him. He was scared of loving her. Scared of losing her. Scared of not being able to protect her. *Pansy* was right.

CHAPTER TWENTY-ONE

Saturday, 3:30 a.m.

"LET'S KEEP OUR FINGERS crossed this statue is dry enough to fire," Kate said, setting the statue of Chaos inside the small electric kiln.

While in Moscow, she'd managed to find a Turkish potter who was willing—for a steep price—to meet them at his studio after their red-eye flight to Istanbul. Ideally, she would've liked to fire this piece in a natural kiln underground, but under the circumstances that was impossible.

"Do we have any other options?" Riley asked.

"No."

"Then we have to take the chance."

"We don't have Belov's statues," she said. "So what's the point in firing this?"

"If having this Chaos statue stalls March for even a minute, it's worth it. I might be in a situation where every second counts. Besides, it can't hurt."

"All right, then. Here goes." She closed the kiln

and fired it up. "In about twelve hours we'll see what we've got."

That was less time than the typical firing process required, but they didn't have any other choice. The flight from Moscow to Istanbul had taken a little under three hours, and they'd gained an hour back in the process, but they'd still be cutting it close. The kiln would be finished only a short while before they were supposed to meet March.

"With any luck," Riley said, "Trace will have Jenny and whether that statue is in a million pieces or not won't make a difference."

They thanked the potter, explained they'd be back when the kiln had finished its cooling cycle and headed back outside to their rented vehicle. They made one more stop, to meet with Angelo's friend and pick up a couple weapons, and then they were back on their way.

"Let's find a hotel and get some sleep," Riley said.

Nothing had ever sounded quite so good, but the prospect would've held more appeal to Kate if Riley hadn't constructed a mental wall between them the moment they'd left the Moscow hotel room for their flight to Istanbul. As if he'd flicked a switch inside him, he'd gone from lover to soldier in the blink of an eye.

Kate glanced out at the bright lights and busy streets as they flew through Istanbul in the wee hours of the morning. The city's climate was temperate, warm and humid even in the fall, positioned as it was amidst so much water. Not only did the mighty Bosphorus River cut the city in half, the Black Sea lay to the north and the Sea of Marmara directly to the south.

In all her travels she'd never been to Turkey, and Istanbul, full of chic nightclubs, busy bazaars and the smells of the sea, was an unexpected surprise, as was the plush high-rise where Riley insisted they stay. With a modern lobby decked out in full regalia for the upcoming holidays, five-star service and panoramic views of the city from every window, this hotel was nothing like the dump they'd found near Rome.

"I want a decent bed and a few solid hours of sleep," he'd said by way of an explanation. "This place should be relatively secure, but I'll get adjoining rooms to be safe. Okay?"

After what had happened between them at that hotel room in Moscow, he was still trying to keep his distance. Too tired to argue, she nodded, but in truth, after everything they'd been through, she wasn't sure she was going to feel safe without him near.

"This is it." Once they reached the sixteenth floor, Riley went into her room first, checking it out. "It's clear," he said.

Kate walked through the door, barely noticing

the red-and-white ultra-lush decor or the vase of fresh and fragrant white roses on the table, and went out onto the balcony. Having flipped through maps and tourist information on the flight from Moscow, she knew exactly where they were.

Located at the top of Taksim Hill, their hotel looked out over the Bosphorus River, the dividing line between Europe and Asia. During the day, ferries, yachts and sailboats no doubt cruised along the wide blue waterway. The lights of a suspension bridge, the largest Kate had ever seen, stretched high over the wavy waters. Seraglio Point was in the distance and even farther, the darkness of the Sea of Marmara.

Normally she would've been itching to explore the city, dotted with domes and minarets as it stretched out before them. But she could barely summon the energy to take off her shoes.

"Kate?" Riley said from the door leading into his adjoining room. "I'll be right through here if you need anything."

"All right." She dropped her bag onto the bed.

"I want you to stay in your room. No matter what, okay?"

She followed him to the door. "Okay."

In about twelve hours they would be meeting March to give him the statues. If Kozmin didn't show, they'd be in deep trouble. One way or another, though, this was all going to be over. She'd either be back in D.C. going on with life, or she'd be dead. But nothing would be as before.

"Kate, what's the matter?"

She glanced at him, her heart racing in her chest. She'd known Riley less than a week and she wouldn't presume to know she wanted to spend the rest of her life with him. But she sure wanted the rest of this night. "I...I don't want to be alone right now."

For a moment he held her gaze. Heat flickered in his eyes.

"No, that's not right," she whispered. "What I want is for you to stay with me."

"Kate, what happened in Moscow—"

She put her hand to his lips. "I know," she said. "You think it was a mistake. You want to protect me from it ever happening again."

"Kate..."

"Don't." She shook her head. "Don't try and explain your ridiculous logic, because I'm not buying it. But I refuse to throw myself at you yet again. You know how I feel. You know what I want. And you know where to find me when you're ready to be honest with yourself about what *you* feel. What *you* want."

She turned and walked into her room. She desperately wanted to shut the door between them in his face, lock it and throw that chain into place. Instead she left it wide open and went into her bathroom to take a shower, forcing herself to be vulnerable. One last time.

Come to me, Riley. Admit you need me as much as I need you.

RILEY HAD TAKEN a frigidly cold shower, gone through his equipment one last time and was now lying on top of the king-size bed in only his boxers trying to sleep. It wasn't happening. All he could think about was the sound of Kate's shower coming through the open door between their rooms. She'd been in there at least twenty minutes. Lathering and relathering. By now, her naked skin had to be almost raw.

He rolled onto his back and stared at the ceiling.

Finally the water stopped. Total silence followed. Several long moments of total silence. *Shit.* Lotion. He envisioned her slathering it all over her arms, her legs, her belly and breasts. Slick cream sliding over clean skin and soft curves.

Stop it, you masochist. Go to sleep.

Right. Not going to happen in the shape he was in. His hands were clenched in fists. His gut was as tight as a knot. And he had an erection as hard as granite tenting his boxers. He flipped onto his side and covered himself with a throw.

Kate's bathroom door opened. In his peripheral vision he saw her pad across the room in an oversize T-shirt. Every muscle in his body went on full alert as he tried to guess whether or not she had panties on under that thing. The scent of something sweet wafted toward him and it was all he could do to breathe.

For a few long moments he lay there, trying to settle. Not only wasn't his body cooperating, but his mind was going full speed thinking about those slender, creamy legs that had passed through his line of sight and what they'd felt like wrapped around him in that Moscow hotel room.

Finally he sat on the edge of the bed and swung his feet to the plush carpet. He ran his hands over his face and glanced at the gun on the nightstand in the hopes that focusing on the work he had yet to do would distract him.

March. Jenny. Focus.

Face it. You want Kate. The only thing that will come close to satisfying you will be having her.

He stood and crossed the room.

ALTOGETHER TOO AWARE of the man lying in the bed no more than thirty feet away, Kate stood at her balcony doors and looked out over Istanbul. A deep breath did nothing to help her find a quiet place in her mind. So much had happened this past week. So much had changed.

She had no clue what tomorrow would bring. She wasn't even sure about the next hour. The only thing she was sure about was that for the first time in her life she was falling in love, and the man she was falling in love with was fighting his feelings with his entire arsenal of weapons. So was she going down without a fight?

Yes. She was. She'd done the right thing in backing away from Riley. Until he accepted—

"Kate?" Riley's voice came from the darkness behind her.

She slowly turned to find him standing in the doorway. The dawn's watery light filtered through the hotel window, illuminating his bare chest. As magnificent as the famous marble statues gracing the museums of Rome, he stood there gazing at her.

She waited.

"I want…" He paused, the air whooshing from his chest. "I want you more desperately than I've ever wanted another woman."

That was what she'd wanted to hear.

"No, that's not right," he whispered.

She held her breath. He was killing her piece by piece.

"What I wanted to say is that…I…need you." Without hesitation, he came steadily toward her. "I need you, Kate, more than I've ever needed anyone. Like water. Air. Like…life."

Stopping only inches from her, he reached out to draw his hand down the side of her face. He tucked her hair behind her ear. "But I still can't make any promises about tomorrow."

"I'm not asking for any. Riley—"

He kissed her, deeply, thoroughly, taking the breath from her throat, the strength from her legs. Her knees buckled and she fell into him and at that moment she knew. This man was going to break her heart. Still, he was all she wanted.

He lifted her, carried her to the bed and laid her back. Kneeling over her, he drew her shirt over her head and tossed it aside. For a long, long while he simply looked down at her, his gaze hovering over her butterfly tattoos.

She held her breath as he touched one after another, lightly, reverently, with the tips of his fingers. When he grazed her left nipple, she arched to meet him. Then his hands were all over her, everywhere at once. From her face to her thighs, her breasts to her belly, her fingertips to her toes. Everywhere his fingers went, his mouth followed, licking and kissing.

Her body was on fire, her breasts tight and achy. Slick moisture pooled between her legs and she thrust upward with her hips to meet him. He ran his fingers up between her thighs and settled there at her center. The moment he touched her, felt her wet swollen flesh, he moaned and dipped a finger inside her warmth. Then his tongue followed, teasing and tasting.

"Riley," she whimpered, writhing against him. "Take me now." She ran her hands through his soft hair, pulled him upward and kissed him, tasting herself on his lips. She wrapped her legs around his waist and arced to meet him.

"Oh, Kate," he groaned as he slowly sank into her. Then he stopped, buried inside her, rested his forehead against hers and gazed into her eyes. "What have you done to me?"

"Nothing more than exactly what you deserve." Smiling, she opened even wider for him, bringing him even deeper.

He sucked in a sharp breath and closed his eyes for a moment. Then, with the kind of restraint and patience she'd never experienced from a man, Riley moved against her softly, sweetly, in and out, again and again, building the tension inside her higher and higher.

"I don't want you controlling this," she whispered. "I don't want you to hold back with me."

"I'm not holding anything back," he said with a smile.

That smile. She ran her fingers over his lips. "You don't need to protect me. I'm not fragile. I can handle you. You won't hurt me."

"I know, Kate. I know. This is exactly what I want." Instead of the reckless sex they'd shared in Moscow, Riley made love to her as if time no longer mattered. He gave her everything he had to give in the most tender of ways.

"Can we make this last forever?" she whispered against his lips.

"Make tomorrow never come? I wish." He gently thrust one last time into her before shuddering to completion.

She hung on to him, coming with him, not knowing what tomorrow would bring and no longer caring. This moment with Riley inside her, his arms around her, his breath mingling with hers, was all that mattered. If she had anything to say about it, she was going to be facing many tomorrows with Riley by her side.

CHAPTER TWENTY-TWO

RILEY LAY IN BED watching Kate sleep. They didn't have much time before the rendezvous with March and he didn't want to spend any more of it with his eyes closed.

Kate, on the other hand, was making up for lost time. She'd been sleeping like the dead, other than a long and luxurious interlude of lovemaking halfway through, for the past ten or so hours. In this relaxed and quiet state with her flawless skin and pink lips, she looked almost angelic. Certainly and unequivocally innocent. A small, feminine noise escaped from deep in her throat, sounding damned close to a purr, and she smiled just enough so that the dimples in her cheeks appeared like magic.

What could this amazing creature possibly see in a beat-up, wrung-out old soldier like him?

But then he imagined her awake, and the sound of her expressive voice and boisterous laughter echoed in his memory. The stern look on her face when she was angry and the way her left eyebrow arced when she was being sarcastic came to life in his mind. Kate an angel? Hardly. She was always opinionated, sometimes cuttingly acerbic and often downright bossy.

She was also strong, sexy and amazingly self-sufficient. She was right. He didn't need to protect her—most of the time, anyway. She'd gone toe-to-toe with him like no other woman he'd ever known. But what surprised him the most was how tender, affectionate and loving she could be. With Ally. With him. The things they'd shared together in this bed came over him in a rush. She was a balm to every bruised and battered piece of his soul, and he couldn't imagine ever again wanting any woman other than this one lying by his side.

As for his age? Didn't matter. She'd been right. He'd been using it as a smoke screen. If anything, the fact that he was older only made them more perfect for one another.

He was so screwed it wasn't even funny.

So now what? If he managed to make it out of this mess alive, then what? When his cell phone rang—a harsh, shrill sound in the stillness—he was almost glad for the diversion.

Kate opened her eyes, and the bubble of tranquillity they'd created in this hotel room popped in an instant. For a moment they stared at each another. The caller had to be either Trace or March. No one else had the number.

He reached behind him and glanced at the display.

"Is it Trace?" she asked, her voice hopeful.

"It is." Quickly he answered. "You got Jenny?"

"Not yet," Trace said. "But we're in position. March is leaving now."

Probably to watch the parking lot.

"Is he taking Jenny with him?"

"No."

"Figures." He glanced at Kate. "All along, he hasn't been planning on handing her over."

"Don't worry, Riley. There are at most two men guarding Jenny. They're going to be outnumbered. In half an hour I'll have her. She'll be safe."

"Text me when you've got her."

"Will do."

Riley clicked off his phone.

"Trace thinks he'll be able to get to Jenny this time?" she asked.

He nodded.

"That's good."

"But there's a good chance I won't know whether or not Jenny's safe before I head to meet with March. I'm going to have to go through the motions, so I'll need that Chaos statue after all. Let's go get it."

In a short while, they were inside the potter's studio. Riley stood in front of the small kiln, holding his breath as Kate checked the gauges. "Can we open it yet?"

She nodded, her face a mass of concern.

Unlocking the door, she swung it open and glanced inside.

"Well?"

"The arm broke off." She lifted the pieces out of the kiln and turned them over in her hand, examining it.

"Can you fix it?"

"Yes." She went to the worktable and found some quick adhesive. Within minutes, she'd secured the arm.

"That'll work," Riley said. "And it looks a lot like the other ones, if you ask me."

"It's the best I can do." She glanced at him.

"That doesn't sound good. What's wrong with it? You were pretty pleased with it before the firing process."

"I was hoping less time firing would compensate for what the electric kiln would do."

He waited for her to explain.

"It's too hard." She handed it to him. "Feel it."

"Like a rock."

"Exactly." Her shoulders sagged. "A piece that's supposed to be as old as this one would be more fragile. In fact, you'd be able to scrape the surface away with a fingernail."

He unwrapped one of the statues he'd stolen from the church near Rome, and pressed his thumbnail against the rough base. If he pressed hard enough, he could easily scrape the surface. He glanced at her. "It's all up to Kozmin now."

"And if Kozmin doesn't show?"

"I'll think of something."

THEY WENT BACK TO THE HOTEL to wait for March to call with the meeting place. They ordered room service and Riley made himself eat to keep up his strength, but the food sat in his stomach like a bowling ball. Kate only picked at her salad, due in part to the fact that March was an hour late.

"Why doesn't he call?" Kate said pacing.

"He's messing with me. Something March loves to do." Suddenly his cell phone rang and he glanced at the display. "It's him."

"Time to get this over with," she whispered.

"Riley here," he said, answering the call.

"Do you have all the statues?"

"Yes."

March relayed an address that Riley wrote down on the pad of paper on the bedside table. "There's a parking garage, but it's under repairs," March explained. "Park on the street. Be there in half an hour."

"Let me talk to Jenny."

"She's fine. Don't worry about her."

Riley paced inside the hotel room. "I want to talk to Jenny."

"I don't have time to deal with this right now. You can talk to her in an hour."

"March—"

"Walk up to the roof of the garage. I'll be watching. Bring the statues. You can talk to her then."

He disconnected.

Immediately Riley tore off the paper and dialed Kozmin's cell number. When his call went directly into voice mail, he left a message, detailing instructions with the address and time Riley would be meeting March. In truth, all Kozmin cared about was getting March, so whether or not he'd be on time to save Riley's ass was anyone's guess. And Riley was guessing not.

He disconnected the call and glanced at Kate.

While he'd been on the phone, she'd dressed and brushed her hair back into a ponytail. She was set to go. "This is it," she whispered.

"Showtime." He nodded. "March wants me to walk onto the roof of a parking garage." Without the protection of a car, he was completely vulnerable.

"I can wait nearby in our rental car. As soon as you have Jenny, you make some kind of a signal, and I gun it toward you."

"Too dangerous."

"For who?"

She wasn't going to listen to reason. There was

only one thing he could do. He walked out onto the balcony and waited for her to join him.

The moment she stood next to him at the railing, he turned toward her and looked into her eyes. What if this was it? What if he never saw her again? "I want you to know, Kate...this last week...I..."

Lacking the words to express what he was feeling, he wrapped a hand behind her neck, brought her toward him, lowered his mouth to her lips and kissed her. Need tightened in his groin. How ironic to find this woman now, at this strange stage in his life, to find someone he knew in his heart he could love.

She groaned and pulled back as if sensing his thoughts. "Oh, no." She shook her head. "You are not saying goodbye."

"I need to stay focused with March. I can't be worrying about what might happen to you."

"That's what you said to Ally," Kate said, shaking her head. "I am not a child."

"Oh, I know that now." He rested his forehead against hers and closed his eyes. Every inch of her screamed wildly passionate woman. "But you're still staying here."

"No! I won't—"

He spun away from her and back into the hotel room. Sliding the patio door closed, he quickly flipped the lock.

"Riley, let me in!" She yanked on the handle and pounded on the door. "Don't do this. Don't you dare do this to me."

"I have to, Kate." He rested his forehead against the glass and formulated his next words. "If I don't make it back, do me a favor and check in on Ally every once in a while. She likes you. She could use you in her life."

"Riley, don't. Don't do this."

He had to get out of here before he started second-guessing himself. "I'll call the hotel right before I head in to see March. They'll let you out."

"That'll be too late," she said. "March expects me there."

"I know."

"Don't do this. Don't leave without me."

Grabbing the bag holding the statues, and one of the guns from the stash they'd gotten from Angelo's friend, he spun around and walked out the door.

"DAMN YOU, RILEY!" Kate pounded the glass. "When I get my hands on you, I'm going to… I'm going to…"

He was going to face March alone. If Kozmin didn't show, he might not make it out of that parking garage alive.

The anger burning in her gut sputtered out. She

rested her cheek against the door and let the emotions course through her. A sense of helplessness settled like a heavy weight on her shoulders. She felt soft and vulnerable and weak.

This was what hours lying in a man's arms making love did to her. This was what Riley did to her. This was what falling in love did to her. Unbelievable. She was falling in love for the first time in her life, and it sucked the big one. Why would any woman in her right mind want this?

Maggie did. So did Shannon. Both strong women. Both blissfully in love.

She took a deep shuddering breath. Clearly it didn't have to be this way. She could be—she would be—soft and strong at the same time. If Riley didn't like it, that was too damned bad.

She straightened and glanced around the balcony. Somehow, some way she was getting out of here. If there had been a table and chairs she could have made short work of that glass door, but there was nothing on the balcony except the railing.

The railing.

Quickly she went from one metal post to the next, hoping to rattle one loose. One way or another she was getting off this balcony, and after this was all over James Riley was going to look her in the eye and tell her he wanted her in his life. Because she wanted him in hers.

CHAPTER TWENTY-THREE

THROUGH BINOCULARS Riley watched the parking lot from the adjacent building. He couldn't see March, but that didn't mean the asshole wasn't there. Pulling out his cell phone, he tried again to reach Kozmin, but the call went directly to voice mail.

He glanced at his watch. Jenny didn't have the time. He had to move, and he had to move now with or without Kozmin.

He placed a call to the hotel and gave them Kate's room number. "I don't have time to explain. Have security go to the room. You have a guest locked out on the balcony."

If he made it out of this alive, Kate was going to be madder than hell at him, but what surprised him was that he was going to want to find a way to make it right. Damn, but she'd gotten under his skin.

This was it. He walked into the parking ramp, took the elevator to the roof, positioned himself at one end and waited.

There was no point in trying anything fancy.

He didn't have the manpower. Either Kozmin was going to fulfill his part of the bargain or he wasn't. One way or another, this was all going to be over in fifteen minutes. Tops.

A BLACK LIMO PULLED ONTO the roof and slowly made its way toward him. Riley didn't move. He could see the driver and recognized him as one of March's men, but that was it.

The limo stopped about thirty feet away, the back door opened and Coben appeared. Two other men followed, and finally March stepped outside.

"Hello, Riley."

"Where's Jenny?"

"Don't worry. She's safe." He cocked his head. "Put the statues on the ground."

Riley set the box containing the statues in front of him and then backed away. Coben came forward and picked up the box.

"Where's Kate?" March asked.

"Someplace safe."

"Predictable. Again."

March's art expert, the short, scrawny man Riley had seen back in D.C., climbed from the back of the limo, and Coben handed him the box.

"Authenticate them, Stanley," March ordered. "After we turn the merchandise over to my buyer, you can collect your fee and be on your way."

"There are only three statues here," Stanley said, carefully examining the contents of the box.

March barely reacted. "Where's four and five, Riley?"

"On their way." *Come on, Trace. Call me.*

"The deal was all of them. Here, now. Or Jenny pays."

"We had some difficulties in Russia. Grigori Kozmin is Vasili Belov's chief of security. But then, you knew that, didn't you? That's why you sent me to Moscow."

"I don't care what kind of problems you had with Kozmin. I need all the statues and I need them now."

"It'll get here when it gets here," Riley said, stalling.

March pulled out his cell phone and dialed a number. "You have until the count of three, Riley. Produce the Russian statues, or my men will start snipping off Jenny's fingers."

KATE RACED THROUGH Istanbul's crowded streets as fast as she dared. Riley didn't think he was going to make it out of this alive. That's why he'd left the car keys and taken a taxi to meet March. Well, she wasn't more than ten minutes behind him. That sliding door had taken her longer than she'd expected to break, but she'd finally gotten a rod loose from the rail and broken the glass. She'd found the address of the parking ramp indented on the pad of paper by the phone and had grabbed a gun on her way out the door.

She turned onto the street where the parking ramp was located. Halfway down the block she found the entrance to the ramp blocked. The garage was under repairs. Too bad. She drove right through the barricade and made her way through the vacant floors, hoping she wasn't too late. For the first time ever, she was hopeful she could have the kind of life her sisters had, and Riley was the key. If he didn't make it out of this mess alive, her piece of heaven would be gone forever. She couldn't let that happen.

A STREAM OF SWEAT DRIPPED down Riley's back, but he stood firm. "You're going to have to make a deal with your buyer. I can't give you what I don't have."

"Not good enough. Get Jenny," March said into his phone even as he glared at Riley. "I don't care if you're having problems! Get her. At the count of three. Cut off a finger. One. Two—"

"One of these statues is a fake," Stanley said.

March turned toward his art expert. "Now, *that* I didn't see coming." He laughed, still holding his cell phone. "How do you know?"

"It's a fair imitation." The man adjusted his glasses. "But typically, on pieces this old, the clay should flake off with the scrape of a fingernail. This one's too hard. That means it's been recently fired."

March turned back to Riley. "Kate Dillon was supposed to authenticate the statues. Not assist you in fabricating them."

"Angelo's statue burned in a fire," Riley said, hoping to stall a few more minutes. "We didn't have a choice."

"Okay, so maybe I can explain that one away. But I'm still missing the two Russian statues!" March yelled. "Cut off a finger. Now!"

Riley's cell phone vibrated in his hand. He glanced at the screen.

Got her. She's safe.

Riley closed his eyes and relief flooded through him. Jenny was safe. That's what mattered most. It might be nice, though, if Kozmin would show so he could get out of there in one piece.

"What?" March said into his phone. Then he shook his head and muttered, "Perfect. Just perfect."

The noise of tires screeching up the ramp sounded through the relative quiet. Kozmin. Riley relaxed. A second later the rental he and Kate had used came barreling onto the roof, raced toward him, and he tensed again. Kate? How had she gotten out of the hotel room so quickly?

Cutting off March from Riley, she skidded the

vehicle to a stop not two feet from Riley and kicked open the passenger door. "Get in."

"I can't."

"I talked to Trace," she called. "He has Jenny." March's men had aimed their guns at her.

"Kate, you shouldn't have come."

"But it's over."

"No, it's not." He wished that he could call it a day and head back to the States with Jenny, Ally and Kate. Buy a house for Ally. Settle down and date Kate. For real. He hadn't been on a date since high school, since Amy. He glanced into Kate's eyes and saw his future reflected there, a future full and rich. And civilian. Maybe he'd even make it to date four with her. But there was one more thing he had to do before he could put this soldier's life behind him.

"I don't understand," she said. "Without Jenny, March has nothing hanging over you."

"March has turned up in my life over and over like a bad penny. I want to be done with him, once and for all."

"But Kozmin—"

"He's not coming. Kate, you have to go!" he yelled. "Now!"

"Tell her to get out of the car," March said.

"Go to hell." Riley walked around Kate's vehicle and headed toward March. "This is going to end between you and me. Kate stays out of it."

Coben stepped between Riley and March. "First you have to deal with me."

"Gladly." Riley kicked the gun out of Coben's hand and landed the first punch. Coben's gut was rock-hard and the blow had little to no perceivable impact. "Tough guy, huh?" This was going to be interesting.

Coben's fist came from nowhere and smashed into Riley's jaw, rattling his head and jerking his neck back. The tang of blood exploded in his mouth, but he quickly threw two more punches into Coben's stomach. This time the man doubled over. Riley kicked Coben's foot out from under him, causing him to fall back onto the concrete.

"That's it!" March aimed his gun at Riley's head. "You're not holding any cards, Riley, so I have no reason to fight you. It's over."

"No!" Kate yelled, climbing from the car and pointing a gun at March. "You shoot him, and I swear I'll kill you."

The sound of more screeching tires pierced the air. Then two more cars pulled onto the roof. Kozmin. Riley took a deep breath as the Russian stepped out of one of the cars. Seven other men followed, carrying AK-47s and semiautomatics.

"What the—" March sputtered.

"Now. It's over," Riley said. "You've made one too many enemies, March."

Coben reached for his gun on the ground, fired at

one of Kozmin's men and rolled for cover. Several shots were fired simultaneously, stopping Coben cold. As Coben's blood pooled around him, the Russians surrounded March and his men. March's men dropped their guns as Kozmin stepped forward. "I told you we would meet again," Kozmin said.

"Predictable enough for you?" Riley called to March.

March glanced back at Riley.

For an instant, regret that it had to come to this swept through Riley, but then the hard madness in March's gaze registered. There was no other way to be rid of this man.

"It's about time," March muttered, as if a death wish had hung over him all these years. Then he spun away from Riley and turned his full attention to Kozmin. "Look, Grigori, I don't blame you for being pissed," March said, holding out his hands in surrender. "But what happened back in Georgia? That was business. Nothing personal. That woman had some information I needed, and there was only one way to get it"

"It's about to get very personal," Kozmin whispered. "Between you and me." He glanced at Riley. "You and your woman can go. Leave the statues."

"That wasn't the deal!" Kate said. "Those statues don't belong to you."

Kozmin took his eyes off March for a few seconds to glare at her.

"Kate. Leave them." Riley dragged her with him
as he backed away. He glanced at March. "Goodbye, David."

March only glared at Riley and dropped his
weapon.

Monday, 2:00 p.m.

"JENNY!" ALLY RACED OUT of Angelo's Athens
home and across the driveway toward her aunt,
almost knocking Jenny over on contact.

"Whoa!" Jenny wrapped her arms around
the teenager. "I'm so glad you're safe. I was so
worried."

"Worried about me?" Ally laughed. "I was with
Dad and then here with Angelo and Nadi."

"I know, but I couldn't help it."

"Are you okay?"

"I'm fine. Good." Jenny cupped Ally's face. "I'm
ready to go home."

Home. Riley watched Ally with Jenny and his
heart clenched. What was he going to do? He still
couldn't stomach taking Ally from Jenny, but he
needed to be with his daughter, for her sake as well
as his own.

Ally turned her gaze toward him as he, Kate and
Trace followed Jenny's path across the driveway

toward Angelo's house. She ran to Riley and jumped into his arms. "Daddy! I'm so glad you're back."

God, she was getting so big. "I promised, re-member?" He closed his eyes and held her for a minute, reminding himself that it was over. She was safe. So was Jenny. And Kate.

"Kate!" Ally cried, slipping out of his arms and moving on.

"Hey, Ally." Kate hugged her. "It's so good to see you again. I missed you."

"I missed you, too," Ally said, glancing at the man standing next to Jenny. "Who's he?"

"This is Trace," Jenny said, hooking her arm through his and pulling him forward. "Trace, this is Ally."

"Hi, Ally. Nice to finally meet someone I've heard so much about."

Jenny glanced at Trace and the shine in her eyes turned a bit brighter. As they stood side by side, Trace's hand touched Jenny's and their fingers entwined for a moment. No one else seemed to notice, but Riley couldn't help chuckling to him-self. *I'll be damned.* He never would've thought to pair up these two, but oddly enough it made all the sense in the world.

"What?" Kate asked, glancing at him.

"Nothing," he murmured. "I'm glad it's all over."

"Mission accomplished," she whispered. "Again."

As much as he ached to see the pain in her eyes, he couldn't talk about what happened next between them. Not yet. First he had to settle things with Ally.

Jenny and Trace headed into the house with Angelo, but Ally hung back. "So what now?" she asked.

"I'll let you two talk," Kate said, taking a step toward the house.

Riley put a hand on her arm, gently holding her back. "Can you wait? I have something to say to you both." The two most important women in his life. He glanced from one face to the other, faces that felt as much a part of him as his own. "I'm retiring from the military." As soon as the words left his mouth, he knew it to be the right call.

No more pansy. Never again.

"It's time for me to settle down." He focused on Ally. "I'm going to buy a house near Jenny, so you don't have to change schools and you can see her as much as you want, but you should be living with me."

"Serious?"

Riley nodded. "Do you want to live with me?"

"You're so stupid sometimes." Ally laughed. "Of course I want to live with you. But what about Jenny?"

"We'll figure it out." He had a feeling the solution would very likely involve Trace.

"This is awesome," Ally said. "I can't believe you're going to be staying in one place. Can I tell Jenny?"

"Sure."

Ally headed toward the door, grinning. "You guys coming?"

"We'll be there in a minute, Ally."

Ally's grin faded as she glanced from Riley's serious face to Kate. "Dad, you and Kate—"

"This is between us, Ally," Riley said, cutting her off. "Give us some time alone, okay?"

For once in his daughter's life, she did what he asked without a fuss and walked slowly into Angelo's house.

For several achingly long moments Riley stood glancing at Kate in silence, not knowing where to begin. What was even crazier was that she had nothing to say. That, probably more than anything, confused and unsettled him.

The past week with Kate and Ally had made Riley question everything he thought he knew so well, and in the calm between when they'd left Istanbul and returned to Greece to get Ally, his life had come back into focus. Not surprisingly, the scenery had changed. What he wanted today was different than what he'd wanted a week ago, but things might have changed for Kate. He wasn't going to hold her to anything she'd said or done while tensions had been high.

"I'm glad you've decided to retire," Kate finally said. "I think you'll enjoy spending time with Ally."

"What about us?" he asked softly.

"I don't want us to be over," she whispered. "You know that."

He knew what she thought she wanted.

He held her gaze, his heart suddenly racing as if a knife was at his throat. "In the heat of things, when lives are at stake, people feel things. Say things." He paused, swallowed. "They do things that are out of character. Emotions are high and they're running on instinct. Adrenaline. But when the dust finally settles everything goes back to normal. Life goes on as before."

"You think what I said to you wasn't real?"

"I wonder."

"You think I'll change my mind?"

"I'm retiring, Kate. My life is in a state of flux. I think that a soldier is always a hero in the midst of battle, but at the end of the day, when he puts down his gun, he's just a man like every other man. Your feelings are bound to ch—"

"No." She stepped back from him and shook her head. "I've heard enough."

"Kate—"

"Now you listen to me, James Riley." She

pointed her finger at him. "I agree. Extreme situations can make for extreme emotions. But it was that intensity that made me see things differently. Shocked me into seeing myself—and you—more clearly. Nothing about that new understanding is going to change simply because there isn't a gun pointed at my head."

She paused, but knowing he'd piss her off more if he interrupted, he kept his mouth shut. And he was okay with that.

"I don't know what will ultimately happen between you and me, but I want the chance to find out," she whispered. "I want to discover what your idea of a real date is, what a lazy Sunday in your arms feels like, what it's like to grocery shop with you. Make dinner. Go for a walk. Watch a movie. If I'm right, I'm going to want to discover you for the rest of my life."

"You think so, huh?"

"I'm sure that I have never felt as comfortable with myself as I do when I'm around you. I don't have to hold my tongue or worry about either hurting your feelings or impressing you. I can say what I want when I want. I can be myself. But I'm not sure I should be."

"What?"

"I'm nothing at all like Amy. That worries me. I can't be…soft. I'll never be accommodating. It isn't in me."

"Oh, you can be soft, all right." He swallowed as he thought of how vulnerable she'd been making love with him. "As for accommodating, I don't want you to be. I'm a stubborn, opinionated brute. What do I want with accommodating? I want someone who can stand up to me. Who won't let me run roughshod over her. Kate, I like you exactly the way you are."

"Are you sure?"

"So help me God," Riley whispered. "I wouldn't change a thing about you. I want a woman who knows her own mind. Knows what she wants and isn't afraid to fight for it." He smiled, felt the first real joy he'd felt in years settle in his core. "You do know your own mind, don't you?"

"That I do." She grinned. "I know I'm falling in love with you."

"Good. Because—and I never thought this would happen—I'm falling in love with you, too."

As he lifted Kate into his arms and held her tight, he caught a glimpse of Ally and Jenny at Angelo's front door. They smiled at one another, wrapped arms around each other's waists and walked away. Retirement was suddenly looking pretty good.

"Do you suppose you can make it to date number four with me?"

"Mmm. You have to make it past date one first.

I should warn you… I'm the kind of girl who likes to be wined and dined."

"Sure you are." He chuckled. "How 'bout dinner and a movie?"

"After what I've been through this past week? Sounds awfully tame to me. Can't you come up with something a bit more…exciting?"

"Exciting?" he whispered, pressing his lips against hers. "All right, Kate. I'll give you exciting."

EPILOGUE

Approximately five years later...

THE EARLY-SUMMER NIGHT was hot and muggy, but the sky was clear and a steady breeze kept the bugs away. Amidst a sea of blankets spread out on the grass, Riley sat on a crowded hillside watching the main attraction unfold before him.

"John Rausch," the announcer said, pausing. "Kaylee Reyerson." Another pause. "Allison Riley."

"There she is," Riley whispered to his middle two daughters, tears of pride welling in his eyes. "See your big sister?"

"Ally!" Sinead, almost four years old, pointed. "I see her. It's Ally!"

"Awee?" Erin's two-year-old eyes grew wide. "Where's Awee?"

"Up there on the stage," Kate said, rocking baby Caitlin in her arms. "See her walking, so tall and strong?"

As Ally marched across the stage, shook the high school official's hand and took her diploma,

Riley's chest swelled. His little girl was all grown and heading off to college.

Well, Amy, I ended up doing okay, I guess. Better late than never, eh?

In truth, he had Kate to thank for these past years with Ally. They'd been good years, too. He and Ally had made up for a lot of lost time, making saying goodbye to her all the harder. How was he ever going to let Sinead, Erin and Caitlin go?

As Ally rejoined the rest of her classmates off the stage, he glanced over at Kate, his wife. She squeezed his hand, immediately understanding the myriad emotions running through him. "You did it," Kate whispered. "She's a wonderful young woman."

"We all did it." He glanced at Jenny, who was sitting on the adjacent blanket with Trace and Riley's parents. Jenny was, of course, bawling like a baby. Being eight months pregnant with her and Trace's second child had her hormones going wild, but she would've cried in any case.

Jenny smiled at him, her eyes bright. "Good thing she's only going to Georgetown, or Trace and I might have had to move."

Trace kissed Jenny's head and squeezed her shoulder.

"What do you think, Mags?" Nick, Riley's brother-in-law, said to Kate's sister. "You ready for this?"

He and Maggie sat on a blanket on the other side of them, along with Shannon and Craig. Their kids—Maggie and Nick's three and Shannon and Craig's two—were off closer to the stage watching the commencement.

Maggie laughed. "If the taste of Tessie's teenage angst is any indication of what we have to look forward to, I'll be ready sooner rather than later."

Nick chuckled. "Actually, Tessie's beginning to remind me a lot of a certain testy aunt of hers."

"Not me," Shannon said, shaking her head. "I was the perfect teen. As my children will be."

Kate grinned, her dimples flaring. "Good luck with that, Shannon."

The family banter continued quietly through the rest of the ceremony. A short while later commencement wrapped up and the crowds thinned.

Riley spotted Ally dressed in her cap and gown, running toward their group. She was grinning as she went from one person to the next, thanking them for coming and giving out hugs. When she finally got to Jenny and Trace, a couple of tears popped up, but the smiles were back when she bent and hugged her little sisters.

She stood and finally hugged Kate. "Kate…"

"There are no words, Ally." Kate shifted Caitlin in her arms and hugged Ally. "I love you."

"Same," Ally said, sniffling.

Then she turned to Riley, studied him for a

moment before she flew into his arms, hugging him tighter than he could ever remember.

"I wish your mom could see you today."

"She can, I think."

"I suppose you're right," he whispered in her ear and tightened his hold. "I'm so proud of you."

"I'm proud of you, too, Dad."

That had never been made more clear to him than at his retirement ceremony not long after he'd married Kate. As his twenty-year service record as a United States Marine had been quietly read, a listing of medals, honors, achievements and decorations, Ally hadn't been able to stop crying. They'd come a long way that day in reconciling any outstanding issues between them.

He kissed her cheek as several of Ally's friends ran toward them. "You ready to go, Al?" one of the girls asked.

"In a minute." Ally glanced at Riley. "Daddy?"

"Go, Ally." *Start your life.*

"I love you."

She spun around, and the new graduates ran off toward the parking lot. As the rest of the family decamped and started toward their cars, Riley glanced away for a moment, gathering in his emotions. He looked back and his gaze caught with Kate's. She held the baby in her arms and her face suddenly turned very serious. "Feels like life is moving at light speed, doesn't it?"

House. Marriage. Pregnancies and the birth of three kids. Not to mention the fact that he'd retired and started a private security consulting firm. She'd set up a full art studio in their basement, so they both had lots of time with the kids.

"Hey," he said, planting a kiss on her neck, "you're not regretting date number four, are you?"

For their first date Riley had taken Kate to a firing range. She'd turned out to be a pretty good shot, too. Their fourth date had been a bit more tame. He'd surprised her by making dinner for her at her apartment. He'd made an offer on a house near Jenny's in Alexandria that afternoon and had wanted to celebrate life, in general. On date number 150, he'd proposed and she'd accepted in a heartbeat.

"Except for that hike up the Appalachian Trail when it rained cats and dogs, I've never regretted a single date with you."

"Yeah, but you look awfully cute wet as a drowned rat."

Riley's heart filled with a love so complete when he looked into his wife's face. His wife. His daughters. Being a soldier had been rewarding, important work, no doubt. But this—being a father and husband—was what defined his new life.

"You were right, you know," he whispered in her ear.

"About what?"

"Everything. As usual."

"Well, with Ally moving out, that means we'll have room for one more."

He laughed and kissed his wife's cheek. "Too late for that. Already did the snip, snip, remember?"

"That reversed itself once, Riley. It could happen again." A sly gleam fired to life in her eyes. "We could try for a boy."

"I think it's clear I was meant to be surrounded by the opposite sex." Because he'd never been happier. He brought the back of her hand to his mouth for a kiss. "You and the girls," he whispered, "are all I want. All I need."

As if taking their cue, Sinead and Erin ran toward him, calling, "Daddy, are you coming?" Each grabbed one of his arms and started climbing on him like a jungle gym.

"Of course I am, you little monkeys." He grabbed them and lifted them in the air. Tomboys, through and through, just like their mother. He blew Kate a kiss.

Chaos times ten had somehow added up to a great new life.

* * * * *

Helen Brenna's next books will be available in August, September and October of 2011! Return to Mirabelle Island and get swept away in the lives and loves of the current residents and a few new arrivals, too!

LARGER-PRINT BOOKS!
GET 2 FREE LARGER-PRINT NOVELS PLUS
2 FREE GIFTS!

◆ HARLEQUIN®

Super Romance®

Exciting, emotional, unexpected!

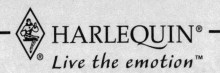